## Praise for *Double Standard*

"A steamy romance about Hollywood power dynamics—it's basically tailor-made for me."

—Erin Foster, creator of *Nobody Wants This*

"I tore through this in one sitting. Smart, escapist, and completely irresistible—with fake dating, a viral scandal, and a stunt double you will absolutely fall in love with."

—Jo Piazza, bestselling author of *Everyone Is Lying to You* and *The Sicilian Inheritance*

# Double Standard

MALLORY THOMAS

831 STORIES

831 Stories

An imprint of Authors Equity
1123 Broadway, Suite 1008
New York, New York 10010



Cover design by C47
Book design by Scribe Inc.



Library of Congress Control Number: 2026937929
Print ISBN 9798893311501
Ebook ISBN 9798893311495

Printed in the United States of America
First printing

www.831stories.com
www.authorsequity.com

For my twin sister, Monica—my very own double—
who was the first person to hear the idea for this story
and who loves juicy celebrity gossip as much as I do.

And for my fellow EDS-ers, who are navigating
life and love while contending with struggles that
are often invisible. I see and celebrate you.

# Double Standard

# I

## ANA

My manager paces my living room reading excerpts from the *Hollywood Star* like a list of charges being brought against me. I sit on the plush, white rug as though I'm a child being told off.

"*Ana and Colt seen canoodling . . . laughing together . . . trying to be discreet . . .*"

There's a moment that comes to mind, the only time I've ever been alone with Colt Haggerty: him walking me to my car after our first read-through of the script, his hand at my lower back, me canting toward him to hear as he relayed a story, waiting for him to finish as I leaned against my car and he reached around me to grab the handle.

Nothing salacious. It seemed chivalrous. Though I can admit, through the lens of someone looking to sell a story, it's how on-set affairs probably start. Someone must've seen us.

"Just . . . how bad is it, Emily?" I ask through gritted teeth.

She winces and continues: "*With Ana Barlow's career finally on the upswing, it seems unwise to make an enemy of Haggerty's wife, Francesca Stella—who happens to be the director on the pair's upcoming film. Ana's diva behavior on the set of her last flick,* Made from Scratch—*showing up late, questioning the producer, ruffling the feathers of her co-stars—overshadowed her work. She'd be smart to avoid a repeat performance, though no one's ever claimed Ana Barlow's intellect is what's driving her success.*"

Emily pauses to scroll, and I get a sinking feeling. "Let me guess . . ."

"They inserted a photo." She rolls her eyes—she's my best friend, after all, not just my manager. "You in that bikini."

I know which one. I got rid of the swimsuit the same day that particular privacy violation surfaced.

She exhales and then reads: "*It's certainly ironic that ahead of playing the titular 'virgin goddess' in* Athena's War, *Barlow can't seem to keep her hands to herself.*"

I sink further into the soft wool beneath me, bringing my forehead to rest on my knees while I knead the muscles at the tops of my shoulders. They're tight, wound up with the weight of being a woman who's constantly reduced to a nice pair of tits. Or maybe the tension is due to my crappy ligaments that struggle to hold up said tits.

Emily plops down on the couch and brings her hands under her chin, her elbows on her knees. She's thinking.

When I press up to my feet to join her, my right ankle

collapses and sends me careening back toward the floor before I can get my bearings. "What the hell?" Emily startles. "Are you OK?"

"It's nothing. Just thought this current shit show could use a rolled ankle for comic relief." The laugh I attempt to force out is strained. It's not funny. There's nothing funny about being unable to trust my connective tissues to hold my joints together, or about the dizziness that greets me when I stand up too fast.

Emily bites the corner of her lip. She's used to my evasiveness, particularly about my body, and she's learned not to push me into sharing more. She makes a move to speak, but I jump in. "God, Em, what'd they say again? *Can't keep my hands to myself?* Like I'd mess around with Colt, especially right before we start filming. I'm not an idiot."

Emily slides down to the rug next to me and wraps an arm around my shoulder. "You know how this goes." Her voice is calm after years of talking me through the ups and downs of my growing public presence. "Tomorrow they'll be on to the next thing."

"But will Francesca? What if she does want me off the project? What if *this* is what it comes down to? Another 'Ana Barlow Sleeps Her Way to the Top' rumor?"

"Hey, remember when someone overheard Rebecca Stone calling you a bitch and it was everywhere, and you were sure your career was ruined? It wasn't then, and it won't be now. I'll ask Marie to start seeding people in the comment section to cast doubt. That'll buy us time until we can meet with Francesca."

I start to sift through all the information I have, like a toddler dumping a bin of toys to see everything at once—noise and mess be damned. All the people involved in this movie. What I know about the filming schedule and location. An idea starts to take shape.

"OK, this is probably a ridiculous thought, but what if . . ." I pause for a moment, trying to sort through the pieces to assemble the plan in earnest. There's a growing dampness under my arms as I consider it, my nerves firing. I know publicity relationships happen all the time. It's part of being in this business. I'd just never considered one for myself before this moment.

"What if . . . ?" Emily replies, drawing out the last word with pinched eyebrows and lips slightly parted.

"What if instead of worrying about the truth, maybe we just feed them another lie? What if we involve Colt's stunt double?" I blurt it out, and Emily raises an eyebrow. My fingers drum on the tops of my thighs. My thoughts dart back and forth between relief and abject fear like a ping-pong ball, unable to find rest. "I could pretend to date him."

In the past, I've avoided making any big decisions in response to press vitriol. But with the stakes of this role, I have to wonder if it's different. And though it probably should feel unsettling to cast myself in an acting role *in my own life*, it feels natural enough. All the lines are blurry, and at this point, it feels harder to try to keep them in focus than to just give in.

Emily looks at me like I have two heads. Definitely confused, certainly concerned. "Your grand plan is to fake date Levi Stephens?"

"I know. I *know*. But hear me out. Anytime I've been with Colt, Levi's been there too. He's green, completely unproblematic, with no actress exes that I'm aware of. And he and Colt obviously look alike. Maybe I was cozying up to this Hollywood newbie instead. Then it's like a redemption story. I could go from homewrecker to wholesome."

Emily nods and twists a thread from the bottom of her shirt around her finger. She blows out a breath. "OK, so let's talk this through. All the way through," she starts. "It's . . . I guess it's honestly not a bad idea. You'd get out from under the Colt rumor, and it could soften your image, which is good. They couldn't call you heartless anymore, and *if* you can convince Francesca, maybe she'll keep you on the project. But you'd also need to convince Levi."

"If Francesca's on board, I can get Levi."

"But if you're found out, they'll say you're whoring yourself out for the sake of your career. That . . . I'm not sure you come back from that."

"They're already saying that, Em. I think it's worth the risk."

# II

## ANA

"You know, I really hate to be having this conversation. But this is my big break too." Francesca sits on the other side of the conference table, and her look echoes mine: polished. Starched and pressed blouse. Hands folded and head tilted to level her eyes at me. In another world, we could have been allies. In another industry, friends. We both know how to present ourselves to be taken seriously, and Francesca doesn't just appear sharp. Her whole persona reads *sharp*.

"Do you know how long it takes to get a major studio to greenlight an action film with a female director? Much less one like me, who's never directed something with a budget over $30 million?" The question isn't rhetorical. "Years. A decade. The chance won't come around again if this production or its stars are trouble for the studio. And frankly, I'm worried you're trouble." She is so focused on her professional reputation, on the sanctity of the production, that she hardly seems concerned with her husband's alleged infidelity. I wish I was more surprised by that.

The air in the room is cold, crisp to the point of painful. I glance out the window, nine stories up, and see cast members and crew scurrying around on the lots below. I have been on lots like these since I was thirteen, practically clawing my way from the plucky sidekick with a five-episode TV arc, to the Disney-Channel-original-movie best friend, to the mid-budget rom-com lead, and now to here, sitting in this room. I swallow against a dry throat before turning to Colt, who's sitting—manspreading—and picking at a callus on his hand. Callous is also what he looks like.

I don't want to beg, to plead my innocence in front of a woman I respect. I can be steely, assured, like she is. I pivot in my chair toward him. "Colt, I'm sure your wife would appreciate your corroboration that there's nothing happening between us. That I am a professional."

"As long as you don't count missing the first fifteen minutes of the table read, sure." He offers a slight nod of the head. An entirely unimpressive vote of confidence from the man who's supposed to be my co-lead. One who *knows* I was held up in a fitting.

Francesca takes the opportunity to hammer the nail into my coffin. "Here's the thing, Ana. It's not just about this story—though I don't love that my marriage is now being called into question." Her eyes slice to Colt, appraising him while he fidgets. There's something in the look, a wariness that catches me off guard. "It's about all the stories that have cropped up in the weeks since casting. Every other day there's some new drama. You have to understand I'm not in a place where I can take unnecessary risks with this production. It would be difficult to replace you this close to filming, but not impossible. I'm wondering if it's necessary."

A rush of shock, prickly and hot, washes through me. It sweeps up my heart and slams it against my ribs in a series of pounding thumps. *No, no, no.* With as much composure as I can muster, I decide to go for it. "I have an idea."

She leans forward, elbows on the table. Her raised eyebrow says, *And?*

"Colt's stunt double for the film, Levi Stephens."

She nods, wariness still radiating beneath the hard set of her eyes, their intensity heightened by her tight, slicked-back ponytail. "The story they're reporting is patently false, but we both know the truth is hardly relevant. Maybe leaning into the idea that, yes, something happened—but not with Colt, with someone who looks like Colt—is the most effective way to quash it. Levi's been at all the *Athena's War* preproduction meetings with us. What if we start spending time together—me and Levi—to make it seem like the tip the *Star* got was wrong?" At this, Colt clears his throat, attending to the conversation with sudden interest. I sit up straighter.

"It's not like there are photos or eyewitnesses to contradict this. He's been in the vicinity every time I've been near

Colt. They look similar enough, especially from afar. We can rewrite the narrative—*and* set up a juicy, on-set love story to attract good press attention and public interest."

Francesca rubs her lips together while she thinks.

Colt looks dubious. "Who's to say Levi will go for it? Did you run this by him before coming here with this cockamamie plan? You can't just volunteer someone to do this sort of thing, especially at their workplace."

Francesca taps her French tips on the table, eyeing Colt before turning to me. "We could sweeten the deal for Levi." The air conditioning clicks off, intensifying the silence as the moment stretches between us. My career dangles from her lips as I wait for her to continue. "The studio will want continuity. If Levi proves himself here, I can advocate for him to continue doubling for Colt in the next installment."

The speed of Colt's head whipping toward his wife makes my own neck hurt.

"It'll be fine." She may as well be patting him on the head. "Ana, you talk to Levi, see what he thinks. If he's in, and if you think he can act well enough to pull this off, we'll move forward."

"Of course. Thank you. I will be—" I stumble briefly over my words, a rare fissure. "*It* will be no trouble."

As long as Levi agrees. And I can make sure Levi agrees.

# III

## LEVI

"So did you grow up here?"

Javier, my Uber driver, doesn't answer me. Maybe it's a stupid question. *I* certainly didn't grow up here—that much seems obvious to everyone I meet in LA. I might have the build for film work, but I don't have the charm. The look I get in the rearview mirror confirms my suspicion. It doesn't stop me from trying.

"I'm a stunt double. That's what brought me here." Yes, I'm answering questions he hasn't asked just to break up the quiet. I've never been good at silence. "You know the Battle of the Gods series? I'm doubling for Colt Haggerty." This intentional name drop gets me a moment of eye contact and a quirked eyebrow. "I know, right? I can't believe it either." It comes out of my mouth with a cautious laugh.

He shrugs as he clicks on the blinker, and my phone rings with a call from Sherry.

"Levi, change of plans."

This is something else I've noticed here: Everyone is

all business. No one has time for a greeting, not even my agent. "I'm texting you an address for Ana Barlow's home. Have your driver bring you there, and we can circle up after. Her manager wants you to meet with her."

I'm quickly learning that utility is Hollywood's currency. *But what could Ana Barlow possibly want from me?* I wonder. Sherry answers before I can ask. "She has a proposal for you, and she promises it's worth your while to show up. I can neither confirm nor deny whether this means sexual favors, and, frankly, I don't care. Just don't screw this up. Listen, I've gotta go. I'm sure you'll do great." I'm also learning that everyone in LA hangs up before I've had a chance to respond.

My experience with Ana Barlow can hardly be called *experience*: I sat across the room from her at the table read a few days ago. She was courteous, though not particularly warm. Where other cast members were happy to introduce themselves and make small talk, she kept to herself.

I try to update Javier with the new address, but he directs me to the app. I take advantage of the thirty-minute drive to google her.

*Ana Barlow in Discussions for* She's All Mine *Sequel*

*They're Just Like Us: Stars Losing Their Cool at LAX*

*'Athena's War' Bets on Barlow and Haggerty*

*What the fck is wrong with AB???*

I click on the fourth link, an r/celebsnark thread from two weeks ago. Immediately, I know it's a mistake. It's full of rants and conspiracy theories—about her love life, her career failures, her diet, all the reasons she looked horrible at a recent red-carpet appearance. To call these comments critical would be an understatement. This is brutal. If she's as closed off as SorryNotSorry87 seems to think, I can't say I blame her.

I swipe up to close the page and put my phone face down on the seat next to me. Trying to learn more about her has revved up my nerves and kicked up my heart rate. Like I'm prepping for a fight scene, not showing up for a business meeting.

The polyester of the seat belt rubs against my neck as I take in a deep inhale, releasing it slowly against the glass window of the Prius as we arrive at a beautiful modern home with drawn shades. Unlike Sherry, I'm not confident I'll "do great."

A few long strides, and I'm knocking on Ana Barlow's front door.

# IV

## ANA

Everything is in place: Two glasses of water, drops of condensation sliding down the sides. Meats, cheeses, fruits, and nuts on a live-edge wooden platter. Small plates. Cloth napkins. Fluffed pillows with a crisp chop at the center. Thermostat at sixty-eight.

From my seat, I survey myself in the mirror above the credenza: Hair smooth and curled at the ends. Soft pencil strokes filling out my eyebrows, undetectable to the naked (male) eye. I tug at my crisp white top to smooth out a crease trying to pop near my waist. I look good. Put together. Persuasive.

The doorbell chimes, and I glance toward the entryway as Emily answers it. My eyes catch on the broad, slightly hunched shoulders of a sculpted man. I take stock: Dark hair with a bit of wave that he rakes a strong hand through. Chinos spread tight across his thighs. Tapered waist hidden beneath a fitted button-down shirt that looks out of place on a guy who's clearly never spent a day in an office.

Levi's been around the studio, but this is the first time I've really looked at him.

*Yes*, I think. *This'll do.*

He follows Emily to the sunroom and stands adjacent to my chair—one of two flanking a coffee table—waiting for me to rise to greet him. Instead, I gesture for him to sit.

"Appreciate you being here," I say. He could not look less comfortable as he folds his body into the small seat.

"Does anyone say no to you?" I clock a nervous twitch at the corner of his lips. He quickly bites down on it.

"You'd be surprised. The smart ones don't. And you're here, so." I raise a brow, wondering how he'll play it.

"Tell that to my dad."

I huff out a laugh, and he stiffens. Seemingly unsure of what to say next, he runs a hand through his hair again, ruffling it to fall across his forehead. It frames his hazel eyes as they track back and forth. My initial read was right—this man is anxious as hell.

"So, Levi, here's the thing"—I say his name intentionally and make sure to hold his gaze—"I am not good at asking for help. I am not good at *needing* help. I would love nothing more than to never need anyone's help for anything at all. But today, I need something from you."

"OK," he replies. Tension lines his face, and his lips are pulled tight.

I bring a hand to the glass sitting in front of me. The perspiration makes the cup slippery under my fingers. "I want you to be seen with me." The words spill out of my mouth before I have the chance to swallow them. *What the hell was that?* I clear my throat in an attempt to button myself back up. "What I mean to say is that I'd like you to join me for a few events so we can be photographed together to sell the press a love story."

Levi raises an eyebrow and tilts his head. He reaches forward to grab a plate and begins piling fruit and cheese on it. It's a relief to see him settle into his chair, to make himself at home here. "Like a fake boyfriend? It doesn't seem like it would be hard for you to find a real one." He doesn't look up as he pops a grape in his mouth. I push the charcuterie board closer to him.

"I don't have the time or energy for, let alone interest in, a real relationship at this point. I want someone for publicity, and I'd like for it to be you." *It has to be you*, I don't say.

He runs his tongue over his teeth—straight enough but with a bit of character, one canine turned slightly in—and drums his fingers on his legs. Contemplating. He considers what I've suggested for a minute before inching his fingers across the table and sliding the meat and cheese back my way. He nods, an encouragement to partake, like if I'm proposing we become a fake couple, the least we can do is share a meal first. "I may be new to Hollywood and how things work here, but I can't imagine that pretending like that is a good idea. We're going to be working together, and I'm trying to get off on the right foot with Colt. Sorry, I can't."

"Colt knows, actually. He signed off on the idea." I grab a few almonds and rustle them around in my palm, the papery skin leaving flakes between my fingers.

Levi's eyes widen. He sets down his plate to stretch his arms behind his head. After taking a breath, he brings his palms to rub against the tops of his thighs.

"I'm sure it's uncomfortable, to know we discussed this before looping you in, but if I can explain . . ."

He stands up, looking over my shoulder for Emily, or perhaps to map an escape route himself.

My mind reels, scrambling for something to say to get him to stay. *If I lose this role* . . . I can't let myself complete the thought. Not when my career is all I have.

My poised, assured persona is clearly not working with Levi, so I decide to slip into another version of myself. To try a different, more physical approach.

"Hey, why don't we go outside? We can walk and talk. Please?" I drop the almonds onto a plate. With a pleading expression, I sidle up against his torso and loop my arm through his. The visible pulse in his neck, blood rushing against muscle, quickens. Both of his eyes flicker closed as though he's deciding whether to entertain this request.

But then his lids pop open, he exhales a breath, and he lets me lead him out the side door.

# V

## LEVI

Sherry was wrong. I am not "doing great." What I'm doing is walking in the gardens behind a house with as many rooms as my family farm's six outbuildings, and I've got a genuine leading lady on my arm who seems to believe that she needs me.

Ana looks up at me—maybe five-foot-five to my six-two—and releases an exhale. "It feels nice to take a walk." She blows a piece of blonde hair from her eyes with the corner of her mouth. Out here, with the sun on her, she looks younger, a bit softer. "I don't tend to relax like this during the day."

I squint at her. "Is that what this is? Relaxing?" A laugh escapes me. "Because I thought I was here for business." It would be great if I could control my mouth instead of blurting out my brain's next thought.

She responds with a sigh, weary and defeated. "Yes, OK. I'd like to tell you more about this . . . thing I have in mind."

I kick at a stick in my path. "I'm not sure I can be of much help."

She takes a deep breath, swings her eyes to her feet, and keeps them there as she speaks. "The *Hollywood Star* published a piece implying that I'm having an affair with Colt. And I'm not, obviously, but scandal sells. That and sex, and the *Star* is trying to sell both." She lowers her voice, even though it's just the two of us. Like saying this is a risk. "I'm weeks away from starting the biggest role of my career, and Francesca threatened to replace me with someone who's less trouble. That's the exact word she used: trouble. Fifteen years of working my ass off—for this."

"She's talking about recasting your role? Shit." The story didn't make it to the top results in my search, but I can imagine it's already picking up steam and will be a talking point, if not *the* talking point, whenever someone discusses *Athena's War*. Finally getting to a place in your career where what you want is within reach, only for someone to get in the way? That's familiar to me. It's rage-making.

"So I had this idea, because there are no photos of me and Colt . . . that it doesn't have to be Colt." She stops walking and turns to face me, finally bringing her gaze to mine. "It could also be you." She holds eye contact, the edge of a plea in her voice. "If we play it right, we could convince the press and everyone else it was always you."

Her scheme finally clicks into place for me. I'm here because I look like Colt. I'm not just some guy. I'm a professional stand-in for the man at the heart of her drama.

"Listen, I know this isn't why you moved to Hollywood," she continues before I can object. "But if you do this, you'll get your name out there, attend a few events, meet some people. Probably gain some respect because a man dating 'up' makes him smart." She adds an eye roll to punctuate the last point, and the no-nonsense woman I first sat across from peeks through. She knows how to get what she wants. Not with me, though.

I start walking again. "Yeah, being seen with you might 'get my name out there,' but this is my first big job. I can't risk being on the next flight home to Ohio. While I'd love to help . . . I'm sorry, but why would I put my career on the line to fix yours?" It comes out harsher than I intend.

"Well, if you can help me with this, Francesca says she'll push the studio to hire you as Colt's double in his next film too. She's a producer on that one, and he agreed to the plan."

"Colt's *next* film?" I ask, brows raised. "So just to be clear: We pretend we've been seeing each other for a few weeks and let people think *we* were spotted together—not you and Colt Haggerty? And then Francesca will ask for me in the next film?"

"Yes, exactly." Ana nods, pulling her bottom lip between her teeth. It pinkens with the contact, and she begins leading us back toward the house. "Assuming you're good at what you do and we can make this relationship feel real."

I understand enough about social media to know that people are quicker than ever to call bullshit on what they suspect are PR relationships, and that makes this a giant gamble. But if it works, this is exactly the sort of thing that would buy me at least another year in the industry, guaranteed. A chance to establish myself. Prove my dad wrong about this career being a pipe dream. And while I'm not sure the plan's foolproof, it seems less risky than most of what's involved in my work.

I could help her with this. It wouldn't be hard. That and, well, I'm a sucker for being needed.

"And if we do this," I start, "how would it work?" I slip my arm from hers and tuck my hand into my pocket. I don't want her touch clouding my judgment.

"Five events together between now and the end of filming for *Athena's War*. Some casual, some not. One in LA with guaranteed cameras, the rest in Nashville when we're filming. We'd be affectionate but not over-the-top. We'd have to kiss for cameras, but we can avoid answering any questions about the relationship because we want to 'respect our partner's privacy.' We'd agree not to be with anyone else romantically for the next few months, publicly or privately."

I nod, enjoying the way her cheeks have warmed with conviction.

"And most importantly, you can't fall in love with me."

At this, the momentum comes to a screeching halt, and so do my feet. "Sorry, did you just say I can't *fall in love with you*?" I choke on a laugh. "Are you worried I might?"

"I don't know. Are you saying I'm not lovable?"

This feels like a test, until she lets a sweet smile slip and gives my side a poke with her elbow.

I can play.

"I'm sure you're very lovable, Ana Barlow, but I'm in no place to test the theory. You've given me a great opportunity I can't afford to screw up. And though you seem lovely, you're not exactly my type." I wink.

Ana scoffs. "Stop calling me by my legal name, Levi Stephens. And also, what's that supposed to mean, I'm not your 'type'?"

"You're blonde and demanding." I shrug. "I'm more of a brunette and easygoing kind of guy."

"Well, lucky for you, I'm not a muscled brute kind of girl."

"Yeah? What's your thing?" My curiosity about this woman sneaks through despite myself.

"If my past is any indication: hot leading men who, when I'm no longer of benefit to them, find someone hotter than me to be with." She rolls her eyes again. "Getting feelings involved has never been good for me."

"Great. I won't fall in love with you, you won't fall in love with me. We'll help each other out and then move on when production is over." I say this casually, as if it's a normal thing people do. I guess here, it might be.

"Do we have a deal?"

I stick out a hand, less clammy than before. "When do we start?"

"At the studio for fittings the day after next?"

"I'd be honored."

She narrows her eyes at me but takes my hand in a firm shake. It echoes the speed of my racing heart. "Save the gushing for the studio. With my reputation, you're going to need it."

# VI

## LEVI

Getting fitted by the costume department at the production office makes me feel like the cows in the milking parlor back home: Shuffled from one place to another, manhandled, spun around, tugged and pinched, then shepherded off to the next thing by a handler. It seems to be business as usual for everyone else—they're having casual conversations about creatine supplements and Los Feliz restaurants like it isn't bizarre to be treated like a human mannequin.

Colt checks himself out in a mirror. We're wearing identical cream-colored tunics, layered and belted at the waist. A costume assistant takes a photo of us from the front, then turns us to the side. "These skirts are something," Colt says.

I shrug. "At least they'll make for easy movement." He responds with a kick of his leg that's more *Karate Kid* than Greek god. It also becomes obvious that he's not wearing underwear. I avert my eyes and redirect the conversation. "So is this the first time you've done a film with your wife?"

His sharp laugh punctuates the air. "Ha! Hardly. Francesca and I met on a set almost twenty years ago. She was an AD for one of the first films I booked. Really young at the time, both of us. Couldn't keep my eyes off her then." His face takes on a far-off look, like he's plugging himself into the memory, before shaking his head and continuing. "She's never directed me before, though. But after two decades of her nagging me incessantly, I imagine it'll feel familiar enough." With that, he leans over and punches me in the arm. A gesture that says, *Women, am I right?*

I huff out a laugh and slap on a perfunctory smile. What's the balance between trying to impress this guy but still maintaining my integrity, exactly? The costumer unwrapping fabric at my waist keeps her face blank, but her discomfort hangs heavily in the air. I fight the urge to apologize for him.

When she steps away, Colt seizes the moment. "Levi, here's some advice you didn't ask for. Sometimes women in the industry can be . . . let's say, tricky. They've spent years hustling for what they want, and they'll do whatever it takes to keep it. Now I'm not saying Ana is looking to take advantage of you with this dating scheme"—he stops to survey the space to be sure no one will walk in on whatever he says next—"but she'd still throw you under the bus in a heartbeat. Keep your hand over your balls, is what I'm saying."

The words come out smooth and land like slime. And he's right that I didn't ask for his advice: Ana and I have a plan here—and we're *both* doing this for our careers. No surprises and no feelings. "Right. I'll, uh, keep an eye out."

"Levi!" Ana shouts when she spots me from down the hall. She is being trailed by her manager, is actively texting, and, based on the production schedule we received this morning, is behind for her fitting. It's a wonder someone isn't trying to measure her while she walks based on how busy she looks.

Our charade starts now, I guess. Do I jog over to meet her? Offer to take her purse? Greet her with a hug or something? I was confident about my ability to pull this off when we agreed to it—I mean, women like me, or at least they do in Ohio—but now? My palms go sticky as I stand here.

"What's up?" I shout back like an idiot. Like I'm fourteen again.

As she comes nearer, the smile on her face makes me think she might actually be glad to see me—or it would if I didn't know she was playing a part. "I was hoping to catch you between your fitting and mine. How did it go?"

"Well, I accidentally saw Colt's balls, so that was something." I need to stop saying shit without thinking.

A laugh, authentic enough that it seems to surprise her, lands between us. Like a permission slip signed by Ana herself, it dissolves some of my nerves. "Well, I'd say that's atypical for a first fitting."

"My eyes can only hope."

Her phone buzzes, and it startles her back to reality. Whispering, "Give me a second," she holds up a finger as she brings it to her ear. "Francesca, hi."

An assistant opens the door to the costume room and gestures for Ana to come inside. She gives them a full palm to say, *Wait.* The assistant stiffens.

"Absolutely, that sounds great. I'm walking into my fitting now, but I'll head over after. Em can pick up my script in the meantime."

Emily, who's been hanging back and watching this exchange with interest, nods.

"Sorry about that. We added a second character development session to the schedule, and trying to find time for eight of us—" Ana waves off the rest of the thought. "Oh, and she's thrilled, by the way. Francesca."

"That you found a time that works?"

"No," Emily jumps in as the costumer beckons Ana. "That you agreed to do this with her."

When Ana moves past me, she grabs my bicep and pauses for a beat, then tilts her head up to mine and brings her mouth to my ear. "This is going to be fun. Promise."

When I pull back to meet her eyes, they flare with something real—mischief, maybe? I'm not sure if she's talking about the film, our charade, or both. Before stepping through the threshold, she turns back. "And Levi?

Does working out together on Tuesday still work for your schedule?"

"You bet." The reply comes with artificial confidence because I don't know what the hell she's talking about. We haven't discussed working out on Tuesday.

But the costume assistant raises an eyebrow and then darts her eyes away from mine, as though she's been caught hearing something she shouldn't. Ana knows what she's doing. That two-minute exchange was all it took for a crew member to assume there's something going on between us. If the gym is where we persuade more people—and those outside of the studio, especially—great. I'm comfortable there.

Now I just have to get comfortable with her.

# VII

## ANA

Even at the most expensive gym in West Hollywood, the smell of testosterone hangs in the air: a unique combination of sweat, preworkout powder, and fragile male ego. While I typically work out with my trainer from the comfort of my home, there is no denying that Swole is the place to be if you want to be seen. Particularly if you want to be seen half-naked and glistening. Which I don't, but I've certainly done worse for less exposure.

I leave the locker room, chrome water bottle dangling from my fingers and bumping against my hip with every step I take. The rhythm of it feels like the ticking of a clock, maybe a bomb, counting down to the moment when Levi walks in and we have to start this performance in earnest—and in public. Except, as I turn the corner, he's already here, sitting on a bench in the lobby. In one hand, his phone, and in the other, a protein shake that he swirls absentmindedly as he scrolls.

He hasn't noticed me, and I give him a once-over. He

looks like he belongs here, and he looks *good.* Perhaps I should've considered, when I decided on the gym for this "date," that he'd show up in a tank that shows off his traps and gym shorts that ride a little too high—a little too nicely—up the cut of his quads. And that I'd be here, staring at him half-naked while wearing painted-on leggings and a sports bra working overtime to cover my nipples. Nipples that are saying hello, that didn't get the memo that this man is a business prospect, not a romantic one. We should've gotten coffee or something that requires full clothing coverage. I cross my arms over my chest and rub my hands along my upper arms to generate some heat. As if that's the issue, that it's cold in here.

"Ana." Levi clocks me and stands up to greet me at the front desk. I straighten, swipe him in, and gesture for him to follow me onto the floor.

"Welcome to Swole." I don't miss a beat as he sidles up next to me. "A gym I've belonged to for five years and have visited probably five times, in part because there are always paps outside." It's like I'm speaking in code, staying cognizant that anyone in this place could be eavesdropping at any time, but still trying to signal to Levi that we'll have the opportunity to be spotted together here.

When a woman tilts her cell phone in our direction, I thread my fingers through his. His warm, rough palm envelops mine, and energy radiates from the contact, sending pinpricks of heat up my arm.

"We'll stay vigilant," he says with a wink. "Where should we start?"

"Why don't you tell me?"

He catches my gaze, and there's a glint in his hazel eyes and a soft smile at the corner of his lips. It etches a small dimple in his left cheek. At the studio the other day, he was stiff—he practically flinched when I touched his arm in passing. Here he looks settled. It makes me think we may actually be able to pull this off.

His palm squeezes mine. "Why don't we start with some stretches?"

He lifts his chin in the direction of a pile of mats in the corner and tugs me gently toward the back of the space. My right hip cracks as I walk, and the sound prompts a visceral response—an immediate flood of hot and dizzying distress that lights up every corner of my body. And it hits me: I let myself get caught up in this charade and made plans to *exercise*, of all things. I thought only about where Levi might be comfortable, and where we could be photographed, and neglected to consider *why* I never come here.

"Wait—" I stop short of the mat he's laid out. "Before we get started, you should know that I . . . well . . ." I stumble, looking for the words. His chestnut brows furrow in concern, eyes stuck on mine.

*What do I say here?*

It would be one thing if I'd practiced sharing the diagnosis with the people I care about, but instead, outside of my trainer, I've chosen to keep it to myself. Emily knows that I'm . . . particular about how I move my body. That I'm careful with what is stipulated in my contracts. But even she doesn't know why. I've spent the better part of my life making accommodations I pray no one notices and doing my damnedest to ensure my issues are no one else's problem. Years of guarding the reality of my needs with the care someone might use to handle a live grenade.

But now I have to tell Levi. Maybe this will be better? Maybe opening up to a relative stranger will be easier. I scan the gym and thank God everyone else in this weight room is focused on their machines.

"So I . . . before we start, I have this thing, and I have to be careful about how I stretch and work out. My connective tissue is crappy—it doesn't function the way it should—and, well, I can very easily dislocate or subluxate my joints, kind of like a dislocation-lite. The condition makes me hypermobile, really flexible, but it also means I can easily push myself too far. It's called Ehlers-Danlos, or EDS. I'm telling you this because I don't want you to think I'm weak or incapable if I need to modify whatever we're about to do."

It all comes out at once, like it was waiting just below the surface. I take a deep breath, pushing air to the bottom of my lungs and back out through pursed lips. Levi gives me a slow nod.

"Connective tissue, so ligaments and tendons?"

"Ligaments and tendons, yes, but also arteries, skin, cartilage—a lot more than you'd think." His eyes are soft.

He's listening intently, and that compels me to say more. "All of them contain collagen, and my body, unfortunately, doesn't produce enough collagen, and what it does make is faulty. This tends to mean everything is a bit floppy."

Before I can stop myself, I remove my hand from Levi's and stretch my forearm to him, palm facing up. I straighten at the elbow, my arm extending well beyond the typical range of motion. Like an upside-down V.

"Ah, so you're double-jointed?" He sets down his phone and shake and brings his thumb to the thin skin covering the crook of my arm. With his fingertips resting on my funny bone, he lifts my forearm up and down, testing. Gently, then rotating. Noticing that I can change my hand from palm up to palm down without my elbow moving at all. He squeezes the joint, massaging the tense muscle just above. I could melt into the pressure, the feeling of his hands on my skin. There's a reverence there. A curiosity that catches me off guard. I hadn't considered that this is a man whose job it is to be very in tune with his body, and that that might affect how he engages with mine.

"This is where you make a sex joke." I force a laugh, pulling my arm from his touch, stepping back from the unexpected intimacy we just fell into. "Something about the benefits of being flexible, or asking if I can lift my leg over my head." To avoid his gaze, I plop down on the mat, lifting my knees to my chest as I sit.

"Is that what people do? Make a joke about how your condition could benefit *them*? I've gotta say, that's not a person *I'd* want to have sex with." He sits next to me, crossing his legs in a butterfly, and winks.

He *winks*.

Manufacturing levity for my benefit on the heels of this bomb I just dropped and then sitting here, his shorts riding up a bit higher as he does, like this isn't a big deal—I don't know what to make of it. Like he heard me say the words, saw my body being weird (that's another thing people say—that my elbows "weird them out"), stored that information away, and moved on.

As an actress, so much attention is focused on my body. My body is a talking point, a casting decision, a challenge for wardrobe, a bit too much up top, a bit too little in the hips for balance. I've been asked to lose weight, look younger, erase my wrinkles, pour my fat into too-small shapewear so a dress "hangs better." I constantly feel like my body is a product to be consumed, whether by movie audiences or by men I date. Levi's looking at me like my body is something more, like it is mine. I can't decide if it makes me want to crawl out of my skin or crawl into his lap.

I hug my knees closer, as if to keep any invasive thoughts out. I clear my throat.

"Let's do something simple." Levi seems oblivious to the way this interaction, no more than a few minutes long, has entirely scrambled my brain. "Just some yoga postures. No weights, no hard conditioning."

"Let's," I say with more authority than I feel. I stretch my legs in front of me and fill my lungs with a deep breath.

I need to get back on track. More action, less thinking. More joking, less wondering if I could ever find as much peace with my body—the way it works, and the way it looks—as Levi seems to have with his.

He stands and holds out a hand to assist me. He moves into a perfect warrior two position, and I emulate him: I bend my front knee over my ankle, ignoring the way the joint creaks, and keep my back leg straight. I reach my hands in either direction, channeling every yoga teacher who's instructed me to imagine that there is a line of energy shooting from my fingertips.

"Look at you." Levi appraises me with a smile. There's that dimple again.

"Shut up and do another pose." I give him a gentle shove on his shoulder to knock him off balance, but he doesn't move an inch.

"Have you ever tried this one?" He moves into downward-facing dog, his fingers stretched and flush on the mat, while his feet shimmy to find the right position. His tank falls, the hem dipping toward his chest to expose a sliver of his abs and the V at his hip bones.

"And there it is, the sex joke I was waiting for." I roll my eyes but don't hate the warmth creeping up my neck. Bending over into my own downward dog, I can only hope he'll assume the redness on my face is from being upside down.

"OK, fair, but not my intention, I swear. How's this one feeling for you?" I notice that his face is equally flushed.

"Feels good," I reply. "Sometimes my muscles get tense from trying so hard to stabilize my joints. It's nice to do some gentle movement like this."

To my right, Levi's eye catches on the windows that run the length of the gym. After a double take, he stands, runs a hand through his hair, and then squats next to me to bring his mouth to my ear.

"There's someone with a camera outside," he whispers. "They're trying to film you. Do you want to go?" His protective act is cute because it's *not* an act. He genuinely thinks this could be a problem for me.

"Levi, of course they're trying to take photos. That's why I chose this place. Let's try to look comfortable together, yeah?"

"Then . . . is it all right if I touch you?" He waits for my quiet "yes" before he rises to his feet, settles himself behind me, and plants his hands on my hips. Hips that are still raised in a pike position, with my ass pointing directly at his waist.

Wow. OK.

"So you're jumping right in, then?" I exhale while pedaling my legs to expend some of the tension that's building between them. He presses in with his fingertips, stilling me. The touch is both assured and reassuring, his confidence meeting my vulnerability like an offering, asking if I'll trust him. Beyond my own understanding, I think maybe I could.

"Just helping you get comfortable." He lifts my hips,

adjusting me slightly to shift the angle at which I'm bent, relieving the pressure on my knees. It's like he knows, without conscious thought, what my body needs. It would feel like more of a revelation if I wasn't so acutely aware of what this position looks like.

"Comfortable with what, Levi? Acting out doggie-style fully clothed in front of a window?" The words come out in a hoarse whisper. A chuckle cracks out of him, and he steps to my side, dragging a hand from my hip along the line of my spine. It makes me shiver.

He crouches down beside me again. "I feel confident they got their shot."

With that, I sink to the floor, grinning, happy to let the blood rush back into my extremities. This man is committed to the bit, which is what I want from him. The unexpected humor? I'll take that too.

As we wipe down our mats, I feel limber in a good way and relaxed in an unexpected way.

"So what's the plan from here? Want to grab some food?" Levi wipes his arm across his brow, baring that same hint of his stomach.

"Oh, well, thanks, but no. I'm not really hungry, and my afternoon has another round of fittings, a meeting with my publicist, and a call about a possible project. And I still need to pack for Nashville. Should we head out?" I thread my fingers through his, but he immediately drops my hand, and for a brief moment, I feel rejection pinching my stomach. Rejection that stings until he swings his arm over my shoulder, pulling me tight to his side.

He's warm and firm, his skin slightly tacky on mine as we head out the gym's front door.

We don't have to wait long until we're greeted by one of my least favorite paparazzi, a greasy guy with a camera around his neck, lens extended fully. "Ana! How's Colt? Is Francesca cool with you two sleeping together?"

I pick up my pace and shield my eyes. He got his shots of us inside; he doesn't deserve anything else.

But Levi stops us, turns, and towers over the guy. "Hey, man, I need you to step back." The photog's eyes dart between us as he withdraws slightly.

Amid my horror, I spiral: *What the fuck is Levi about to say? I should've prepped him to stay quiet.*

"She's not with Colt, she's with me. Are we clear?" He squeezes me closer as he says it, and this is not the gentle, playful Levi of earlier. This version of him is authoritative, possessive even.

"We look alike—Colt and I. That's kind of my job. But you and your second-class, story-selling friends don't get to mistake him for me and drag her into this. So go sell those photos you took inside with my name attached. Levi Stephens."

Well, I guess that's one way to get the ball rolling. I focus on keeping my expression as stern as possible.

I bring a hand to Levi's chest, and his heart is pounding. From nerves or the anger he's projecting, I'm not sure, but it's an easy opportunity to double down on the ruse, to comfort him in front of this sleazeball. "Babe, he's not worth it. Don't waste your energy."

The photographer twists his lips into a smarmy grin. "She's right, man; I don't give a fuck. They can say whatever the hell they want, and that's *your* problem, not mine. Good luck in the industry, buddy. Start by learning how it works."

"I'll take that to heart." Levi turns us away.

We're heading toward a black car. He drops his palm to my lower back and ushers me into the back seat, the faint click of the man's shutter disappearing as he closes the door behind us.

"Where to?" the driver turns around and asks.

"Sorry," Levi says to me. "I shouldn't have pushed you in here. I got caught up and wasn't thinking." He brings his hands to his hair and tugs at the ends. Sheepish, almost. "Did you drive? Did you park in the lot?"

"After that performance, you can direct me into all the cars you want. Francesca is going to love seeing what comes of that."

His hands fall from his hair as his eyes slice over to mine. "You think that was good enough?"

"I think we'll see those photos circulating in hours. Just in time for us to bring this show on the road."

## CELEBS WEEKLY

### Who Is Levi Stephens? Five Things to Know About Ana Barlow's Mystery Man

By Celine Arnold

Here's what we know so far about Levi Stephens, the newest guy to catch the blonde bombshell's eye.

1. **He's from Ohio:** Hailing from the tiny farming community of St. Sebastian, Levi is one of four children born to Michelle, a stay-at-home mom, and Paul Stephens, a dairy owner. As the youngest and only boy, Levi was the apple of the family's eye.
2. **He's a stuntman:** From Levi's *spirited* outburst that made the rounds online, we know he's been cast as Colt Haggerty's stunt double on his (and Ana's) upcoming action flick, *Athena's War*. This appears to be his first major credit and is how the pair were introduced.
3. **He's 27 years old:** Levi doesn't fit Ana Barlow's typical mold. Based on school records, Levi appears to be two years her junior. Though Ana may not be his usual type either: Yearbook photos show him frequently with a brunette who lacks the generous curves our starlet is known for.

4. **He's a gym junkie:** Spotted at Swole last week, the pair worked out together, with Stephens assisting Barlow with one of her downward dogs. We didn't peg him as a yogi, but it looks like he can put those muscles to use outside of leg day.
5. **He's chivalrous:** Opening doors, leaving generous tips, and keeping eager photogs at bay, this Hollywood transplant hasn't forgotten his Midwestern manners. If the man's trying to impress one of Hollywood's rising leading ladies, we have to admit—it seems to be working.

# VIII

## LEVI

The hum of the plane's engines is trying to lull me to sleep. The oversize leather seat I'm in and the blanket that's definitely *not* from Basic Economy aren't helping. But I'll be damned if I miss the chance to get in good with Colt. Four hours next to him while flying private on the way to Tennessee, where we'll be for the next eight weeks, is an opportunity I can't miss.

"And that's when the DP told the crew that they had accidentally deleted all of the prior day's work," Colt says with a laugh, lifting a lowball glass filled with amber liquid to his lips. A matching glass sits on the wood-paneled table to my left. Colt passed them around like he was starting a fraternity and booed when one of his co-stars politely declined.

"So you had to film the entire day over?" I'm edging myself into a conversation I have no real context for, to show him I'm attentive. Succeeding in this role and securing my next will be easier if Colt can put in a good word with his wife.

"Yep. Had to call back some of the bit players who'd already gone home and cast a full new set of extras. Cost the production seven figures to fix that mistake."

"Who eats that cost?"

"Frannie!" He calls to Francesca, one row ahead on the opposite side. She straightens her button-down before looking our way, her eyes dull and joined by a half-frown. She's annoyed to be pulled away from talking to Ana, who's sitting next to her.

"Yes?"

"The day we refilmed for *Galaxy's End*—who paid for that? Levi's asking."

I catch Ana's gaze when he says my name and, God, she looks so comfortable here. At ease in a world as foreign to me as it is familiar to her. She tilts her head and pulls her lips into a soft smile as if to say, *You good?* I nod and return the gesture before grabbing my glass for a drink. The whiskey burns on the way down, but I don't miss the way she watches as I swallow, which warms me nearly as much.

"Production has a budget that includes flexibility for unforeseen issues." Francesca pulls my attention back to the conversation—my task here—and away from the cut of Ana's shirt, which sits tight across her waist and hangs softer over her shoulders. Francesca waves off Colt. "Now if you'll excuse me, I'm going to return to chatting with Ana about more interesting things than film budgets."

"What could be more interesting than what I have to say?" He throws her a megawatt smile.

"We're commiserating about how to deal with men. Ones like you." She turns her gaze to me and holds eye contact. "Actually, like you too, Levi. We all saw the photos from the gym. You don't mind getting handsy, do you?" She nudges Ana with her shoulder, a smirk on her face, as sweeping heat rises on my neck. I can tolerate the embarrassment given how pleased Francesca looks about the recent coverage. When I smile and take another drink, she nods in approval. Whatever she was looking for me to do, I must've done it.

Colt, oblivious to the whole silent exchange, slaps me on the shoulder before raising his glass to Francesca. "I love ya, babe. To fifteen years happily married, and eighteen overall." This prompts a laugh from everyone, and my ears home in on Ana's. It's light, but also bottom-heavy, like a bubble dripping with extra solution. There's more substance to it than it seems, if someone's willing to look beyond the beautiful part.

"What was I saying?" Colt motions for an attendant to top up his drink. "Thank you, beautiful." He turns to me. "Isn't she beautiful?"

I stay silent given that his wife and my (supposed) girlfriend are sitting right there. I wait for someone to call him out, but no one does. Apparently when you have this level of success, you can get away with it.

"Oh yeah, so the situation with the DP. It all worked

out, like Frannie said, but they won't be invited back to work on one of our productions. We don't do second chances."

He says it casually, but it rings like a warning. "Seems perfectly reasonable to me," I say, clinking his glass before we both sip.

He gives me a nod, and it's enough to make me think he's starting to like me. And based on the bits of conversation I'm picking up, Francesca is warming to Ana.

We haven't started filming yet, but so far, everything is going according to plan. When we land, the next phase starts: Keep everyone happy, and don't make mistakes.

# IX

## ANA

Tennessee is *hot*. What do they say about humidity making it worse? Whoever they are, they're right. Standing with the rest of the crew in the mid-morning sun, my hair is growing bigger by the minute. Tony, the eager tour guide for our mandated orientation, is giving us the history of the city's life-size replica of the Greek Parthenon, the site that made this the ideal shooting location for *Athena's War*.

"In 1895," Tony says into his headset as we walk along the structure's concrete pillars, "Nashville decided to take its nickname as the 'Athens of the South' literally and began construction on a copy of the ancient temple. Although originally built to be temporary, the Parthenon quickly became a permanent fixture, and to this day, it represents our city's commitment to educational and artistic ideals."

Levi bumps his shoulder against mine. "What would be ideal is a cold pop right about now."

"Did you just say 'pop'? As in soda?"

"Nah, I don't trust people who say 'soda,'" he whispers back. "So you better tell me now: Can you get on board with pop?"

"Maybe we skip pop and daydream about lemonade. Less controversial."

"You just called it pop." His grin is as wide as it is smug.

I pull a face but find myself drifting closer to him, itching to make contact. To touch his arm or tuck the tag into the back of his shirt and graze his neck as I do. *This isn't what "acting" attracted to someone feels like*, I think, but it doesn't stop me from reaching behind him and grabbing the phone out of his back pocket. I decide it's a nice hint at the comfort between us. For the sake of the cast and crew.

"Selfie?" I say as I swipe open the camera. "Ready?"

He grabs the phone from me, raises it, and flips to the front camera. I had envisioned something more considered—find our angles, get the light right—but he tilts his head toward me and snaps before I can protest. He hands it over for my approval: his one-dimple smile, my face in profile looking up at him expectantly, a sun flare that bathes us in just enough mystery. It's perfect. I ask him to text it to me so I can post it.

There's a lot to hate about social media, but at least there I can control my image. This shot of us, with a coy, throwaway caption like *Athena at the Parthenon*, will get my six million followers into a buzz about the two of us. And if the comments go south? Emily can turn them off.

I've almost forgotten about the tour until I hear Tony clear his throat. "For decades after its opening, our Parthenon was missing its Athena. Any guesses about how long it took to craft our goddess?" He points to a towering golden statue inside, like we might miss it. "Eight years! That's how long this *monumental*—pun intended!—feat took to complete."

"Monumental is right!" Levi's voice is a bright burst, and even I know him well enough to know that he's kissing ass. But Tony's eyes grow soft. There are roughly twenty-five cast and crew members in his midst, mainly lead actors and those doing stunts, and I can't imagine he will be thrilled to watch them scale these pillars a few days from now.

Warmth, less harsh and more fragile than the sun searing my skin, blooms in my chest. I'm starting to believe Levi genuinely wants to make people happy. And if I wasn't so jaded from years in a job where people are only kind if they want something from you, I'd find it endearing. A tiny part of me still does, and that feels dangerous, like a liability. Instead of dwelling, I catalog the trait as a strength we can use—to win people over for us. For me.

"Suck-up," I whisper. Levi flashes me a smile, and the singular dimple in his cheek makes a fleeting appearance.

"You're just jealous Tony likes me more than you."

"I don't need him to like me. I need this to wrap up so I have time to shower and do a final read-through before the event later."

"Is it normal to do a meet-and-greet before filming starts?"

"It's a first for me, but according to Francesca, it was part of the deal with the city, in exchange for us filming here. You'll have fun—children's hospital visits, where showing up really means something to the kids, are my favorite."

He nods with his lips pulled between his teeth, like he's mulling this over. "Will there be photographers there?"

"Outside, most likely, though it'll probably be fans instead of paparazzi. We should be blissfully press-free during the visit, though the guests could say anything to the media afterward."

I'm speaking in code again. I give him a look to say, *So you better act like my boyfriend.*

Levi slides an arm around my shoulders, a silent acknowledgment that he's picked up the message. After another few minutes walking up and back down the stairs in front of the Parthenon, Levi glances at his watch. "Hey, Tony! What's the ETA on wrapping this up?"

Tony shrugs and keeps walking. Francesca, who's been trailing behind him while taking calls and occasionally pointing things out to various production members, shoots Levi a look and then me an eye roll. After seeing our fake dating scheme in action, her iciness has started to thaw. Now, after the plane ride here, our rapport includes acknowledging the shenanigans of the men we work with.

"I tried," Levi says.

"See you at 3:30. And be ready to smile so big your cheeks hurt." I slip out from under his arm as I peel off from the group.

"Am I ever *not* smiling when I'm around you?" he replies with a shit-eating grin, and come to think of it, I haven't seen his nervous, scrunched-up face since that day at the studio in LA. Either he's a better actor than he gives himself credit for, or he's actually enjoying this game we're playing. As I turn toward the parking lot, a devastating thought takes hold: I am enjoying this too.

# X

## LEVI

"Coming!" I hear Ana shout from behind the heavy-looking wood door I knocked on just a few seconds ago. The home she's staying in has stucco walls, arched windows, and burnt-orange Spanish tiles lining the roof—nothing like the downtown rental apartment I was assigned by the production company.

She greets me with a huff, twisting up her blonde hair before securing it with a clip. Though I've been told the event tonight is casual, I'm pretty sure it's not joggers-and-a-tee casual. But here she is, standing in front of me in a T-shirt that's ridden up with the lift of her arms to bare a soft sliver of skin above her waistband. I assume it's soft. The impulse to run my palm across it—to confirm—sparks in my fingertips. *Nope.* I shove my hands in my pockets instead.

"I told you to get here at 3:30 p.m. It's only 3:22. I'm not ready," she says.

"On time is late, and early is on time." That's the only

acceptable way to operate on a farm, and it's the only way I've ever known how to be. She crinkles her nose and shoots me a scowl. It would be threatening if she weren't short enough for me to use her head as an armrest. Or if I wasn't so charmed by the smile lines that appear around her eyes when she squints.

"Just letting you know I'm here." I raise my hands in front of my chest in mock surrender. "I'll be in the car. Come on out whenever you're ready."

I jog back to the driveway, ducking to take a seat in the Chrysler directly behind Edwin, my assigned driver and an increasingly familiar, increasingly comforting presence. Having a private car isn't something I expected when I took this job, but it's becoming convenient, as the public's interest in my relationship with Ana—and in me—has grown. Our first formal appearance together at this event tonight is likely to intensify it.

Meanwhile, my agent's inbox is full of opportunities I wouldn't have been considered for a few weeks ago. Interview requests, a brand sponsorship, modeling calls—Ana was right that simply existing in her orbit would raise my profile. I can only hope I've been half as helpful to her.

Edwin turns around in the driver's seat to face me. "Let me be the first to tell you that waiting on a woman never ends. I've been at it for years."

"Oh, this isn't a—" I stop myself from saying *a real relationship* because it's supposed to look like one. For all I know, he could take something I tell him and sell it as an insider story. "I'm happy to wait," I go with instead, just as my eyes catch on Ana swinging open the front door.

"Ready!" she calls as she crosses the threshold, transformed from cute and casual to downright stunning in fitted jeans, black heels, and a silk blouse that hugs her waist. I'd have to fight my gaze from lingering there if it wasn't already trained on her mouth, which is painted bombshell red. Her hair falls in waves, framing her face, and she tucks a strand behind her ear. If I wasn't sure before, it's now clear that Ana Barlow is completely out of my league, even as my fake date. That she'd voluntarily spend time with me is one hell of a story to sell, but lucky for us, the public seems to be buying it. I need to make sure *I'm* still buying it: The way my pulse kicks up as she approaches the car doesn't feel fake.

Edwin hops out of the driver's seat to open the back door, and I slide across the cool leather to make room. "That was fast."

"Fast and easy is what I'm known for." She laughs, but it's joyless.

I grab her hand, ducking my head to find her eyes. "New rule," I say as the car pulls out of the driveway. "No self-deprecating. We've got twenty-five minutes—maybe more—and the deal is we only say nice things about ourselves. OK?"

She taps a finger against her lips and narrows her eyes. "Last I checked, I was the one making the rules."

I shrug. "Then we'll stick to the negative stuff. If that's

what you want." She tries to interject, but I keep going. "I'll start: I left for this job without saying goodbye to my family. Without telling my dad—who expected me to help with calving season—and I think I should feel guilty about it, but I don't."

"*That's* what you're going to lead with? Not something easy like, 'I'm a terrible person because sometimes I leave the gym without wiping down the bench'?"

"One, I always wipe down the bench. I'm not a monster. Two, you shared something vulnerable with me on our gym date. Figured I could return the favor."

She nods slowly, her eyes tracing my face like she's trying to read whether she can trust my intentions. Her wariness reads like armor, and I'm sure it's necessary after years of working with people who act for a living. I wish she knew she doesn't need to do that with me.

"Well, go ahead, then," she replies. "Tell me about your family baggage and how you ended up here."

Somehow, in this odd arrangement we have, sharing my mess feels like a win when she's the one listening. "You know the story—small farming town, three sisters, blue-collar parents."

"Ahh, yes, Mr. Americana. That's what they're calling you, you know." Her smile creates a pull in my chest, just under my collarbone. I absentmindedly rub a hand there to soothe it.

"Is that so? I guess I'll take it, though I wouldn't say my upbringing was quite that perfect."

She raises an eyebrow in question. I lean in her direction, bring my hand to her leg, and rest my palm on her thigh before continuing. It's for Edwin's sake, I figure. For when he catches a glimpse of us together in the rearview mirror.

"I was the kid who was always climbing on things, jumping off stuff, injuring myself by being reckless . . . and there is a ton of opportunity for recklessness in the country. My mom and dad put me in karate when I was seven to burn off some energy. And by 'karate,' I mean a big-city guy married the daughter of a local farmer and taught a few of us how to fight in a converted shed out back." I grin, thinking of Don and the group of scrappy boys he tried to rein in.

"My parents must've assumed I'd grow out of it," I say, "this propensity to throw myself around. But instead, I pushed harder. I set up an obstacle course in our backyard. I racked up broken bones and sprains, while they racked up medical bills. They were completely exhausted by me, I'm sure."

"And they didn't want you to do this professionally, I'm guessing, even though you clearly have a talent for it?"

"No. They had a whole life laid out for me: Marry my college sweetheart, apprentice under my dad, take care of the house, and inherit the business one day. The true Americana experience." Even joking about it has dread creeping into my chest. "And it's not just that I didn't do any of that, though I know it hurts them. It's also that they worry about me. The whole reason I have a job is because stunts are too dangerous for actors to do. They think if I really love them, I would choose something safer. I wonder, if they really love me, why they can't be more supportive."

Ana slides herself closer, shifting into the middle seat and resting her hand on top of mine on her thigh. The warmth of her fingers pressing into my skin radiates straight to my groin, and I take a deep breath. "If I can establish myself, secure this next contract Francesca's offering, part of me thinks they'll finally get it. Maybe they'll realize I wasn't meant to be in Ohio forever."

"Levi. I think you're exactly where you're supposed to be."

Something in me cracks open at her words. The validation, encouragement. After years of fortifying against people's disappointment, I respond the only way I know how: with humor. "A simple country boy who has no right to be with a woman who looks this good?"

"You know what, fine—I endorse your rule: No self-deprecation."

Our cast is going room-to-room at Vanderbilt Children's Hospital, greeting kids who could not be more excited to meet the stars of the newest Battle of the Gods movie. The pitch was that we'd bring some light to a heavy place by doing these visits, but the concept is fundamentally wrong. I am certainly getting more out of this than they are.

I can't assume the same for Colt, who looks like he'd rather be doing anything other than holding Francesca's hand and making small talk with the kids and their parents. He catches my eye and gives me an upward nod, that universal, unspoken sign between guys that says, *Solidarity, man.* I offer a weak smile in return. Meanwhile, Francesca seems as enamored by Ana as I am tonight, watching her command every space we step into, and giving her a different sort of nod—one of respect and approval.

"Ready for this one?" As Ana approaches the next door, she threads her fingers through mine, and her thumb traces circles on my skin. Holding hands feels natural now, comfortable in front of strangers and our coworkers. It's a relief to have her confident presence by my side. And whether it's an act or not, it feels like she likes me here too.

I grip her palm a bit tighter as we enter a room with "Goldie" spelled out in a collage on the door. The space has been transformed from sterile into something else entirely. It's covered with pictures, flowers, and balloons that bat around as the fan blows, bumping against each other and me as I watch Ana approach the bed.

She pulls a chair up to the side that has the rail dropped and introduces herself. "Hey, friend! I'm Ana. OK, you *have* to tell me about these braids. Did you do them yourself?" Goldie, who looks to be about twelve, lights up like a firework, an explosion of energy in the room that sparks the smiles of everyone else—her parents, her younger sister, the nurse monitoring her vitals. Within minutes, Ana has turned in her chair, and Goldie's hands are in her hair, weaving the strands together.

Seeing Ana like this pushes my heart into my throat. Here she is, managing her own medical issues, connecting with patients like she's their favorite older sister. Soft and warm—that's who Ana is here. She's dynamic. She really *sees* people, and they come alive under her attention. She's not hard and cold, like the public treats her. If only they could see her like this. And yet, I have a feeling that she wouldn't actually want that. That this side of her is reserved for those who deserve it. Based on her encouragement in the car, I'm starting to think I might be one of them.

The thought makes it hard to swallow, and I don't know what to do with that.

Ana flips a braid behind her shoulder and knocks me out of my thoughts. "Any last-minute requests, Goldie? Want us to sign anything before we go see your neighbor?"

Goldie smiles before twisting her lips to the side as though she's not sure she should say what she *really* wants to say.

"C'mon, Goldie," I prompt. "Now's your chance. What can we do for you?"

She turns to Ana, her energy quieter now. "This is silly,

but I know you're here with your boyfriend," her eyes dart over to me and then back, "and I'm wondering if you guys could recreate that famous scene from *She's All Mine* with the kiss and dip? If I put it on Snap, my friends would lose their minds."

The moment Goldie's referring to is from one of Ana's first big roles—the only film of hers I've seen, in fact, years back with my college girlfriend who wanted to go on opening night. It's the kind of rom-com that has found a new audience thanks to streaming. It probably has an abysmal Rotten Tomatoes score but is the subject of thousands of fan accounts.

"Oh, well, Levi wasn't a part of that film, so I don't know if . . ."

"Of course we can," I interject. It wouldn't be hard. And who am I to turn down a girl who has limited chances to impress her friends when she's stuck in a hospital bed? If Ana's in, I'm in.

"Well, OK, then." Ana nods, standing from her chair and walking over to me. "Better get your camera ready, Goldie."

With cautious steps, she approaches me. The others in the room move to line the walls, opening up space at the foot of the bed. "Sorry," she mouths as she gets close. I shake my head. There is nothing to be sorry about.

"Good?" I ask quietly. She nods.

I move in a blur. My arm wraps around her waist, my

hand grips the soft flesh of her thigh, and she hinges back, her braids grazing the floor at full tilt. Her hips press flush to my body, and my blood rushes south, heat and need building as we touch. I know this is for show, my brain knows it's not real, but my body only understands that she's pressed against me and that I *like it*. I lean forward and bring her to me, her breasts grazing the plane of my chest, and then her mouth is on mine.

I feel it everywhere. Warm, full lips notching between my own, the beat of her heart, the thrumming of mine, a soft sigh escaping her throat when we make contact.

No one else could've heard it. That sigh was just for me. Or, if not, it was in spite of her and this plan and what we're supposed to be doing here. She sinks into the kiss like a person might sink into a warm bath. Like it's comforting, equal parts relief and release.

I soak it in—breathe her in—until I'm fully submerged too. This kiss has no business being this good, not for the purpose of a twelve-year-old's Snapchat bragging rights. But I'm not complaining. I'm not stopping either.

In the background, someone whistles and says they expected Ana to refuse the request. Someone else agrees. They're surprised by how kind we are.

Ana stiffens at the exchange and pulls away. When I bring us upright and release her, her lips curve into a guarded smile. She draws a thumb to my mouth to wipe the remnants of her lipstick from my face.

"You did good," she says, a flush on her cheeks that wasn't there before.

"We did good." I center myself with a deep breath before turning to Goldie. "Think that'll do?"

The squeal she lets out is her answer.

As expected, a group of fans with phones is waiting outside the hospital as we approach the exit. Sensing an opportunity, Ana pulls me toward the automatic doors.

"The car won't be here for another few minutes," I say, having just gotten in touch with Edwin.

"I'm not worried about the car." She gestures ever so slightly in the direction of the onlookers. "Why don't we give them what they want so they'll take off? So that they're gone when these families leave? If we give them the picture, my guess is they'll pack it up."

With that, she marches us through the glass doors, under the porte cochere, and behind a pillar.

"I thought we wanted to be seen?" I whisper with a chuckle.

"We want them to *think* they caught us." She wraps her arms around my waist and lays her head on my chest like we're a regular couple stealing a moment. I can't help but rest my chin on her head, breathing in the coconut scent from her hair.

"You were incredible in there," I say, feeling the weight

of her soften against me as she relaxes into the hug. Her arms grip me tighter.

"Are you kidding me?" She looks up, green eyes bright. "*You* were incredible in there. That dip? Do they teach dance moves at stunt school?"

A laugh bursts out of my chest. "No, that was pure improv." Before I can stop myself, I lean down and kiss her forehead. Maybe it's for the fans. Maybe it's because it feels so damn natural. Or maybe I need her to stop looking at me like something a bit too honest is starting to happen here.

Before I have a chance to analyze further, Ana pushes up on her toes, loops her arms around my neck, and pulls my lips to hers. On instinct, my left hand slips to her lower back, my right to cradle her jaw. It's not the same showy kiss we had earlier—this is deliberate, searching. The swipe of her tongue urges my mouth open. A groan escapes me when she rolls her hips against mine, and I answer with a playful tug of one of her braids.

"Be good, Barlow," I whisper against her lips. She pulls away just enough to meet my eyes, a spark of challenge in hers.

"I'm always good, Stephens."

The sound of our ride approaching steals the moment, and Ana places one last kiss to my lips, chaste by comparison, before turning to walk to the car with her hand pulling mine.

*The show of affection was just for the cameras.* That's what

I tell myself, until she looks at me over her shoulder, a soft smile pulling at her cheeks.

"Unless I don't want to be good," she says. "And with you, I'm not so sure."

I open the door for her and put my hand on the roof of the car to steady myself. *Breathe.*

## THE NASHVILLIAN

### *Athena's War* Comes to Town, Brings Star Power

By Billy Slater

The landscape of Vanderbilt / West End has changed with the arrival of the cast and crew of *Athena's War*, the latest installment of the Battle of the Gods action movie franchise. Filming began this week at the Parthenon in Centennial Park, with additional plans to shoot downtown at Bicentennial Mall, the Engrel estate in Williamson County, and a specially built soundstage in East Nashville.

Director Francesca Stella confirmed to *The Nashvillian* that shooting will occur over eight weeks and that they are working with local authorities to minimize disruptions for residents. Those who live near a filming location should expect occasional road closures and/or delays.

While the film's requirements have already created logistic challenges for some residents, Mayor Teddy O'Connor believes the movie will be good for Nashville, stating, "We are thrilled for the economic benefit to our city, plus the expected increase in visibility and tourism that it will bring."

And of course, some locals are hoping to spot the

film's stars, Colt Haggerty and Ana Barlow, during their time in town. While their working days are long, both have been seen supporting area restaurants as well as attending the Vanderbilt Children's Hospital Reach for the Stars fundraiser.

Mayor O'Connor encourages residents to give the *Athena's War* cast and crew a warm Southern welcome and to help make them feel at home.

# XI

## LEVI

We're mid-hand-to-hand combat when Francesca's voice echoes across the soundstage. "More pankration, less boxing!"

Prior to this film, I would've guessed that pankration was a type of pastry, not an ancient martial art. Now we all know better.

"Levi, get lower so you can drag him down by the waist. That will help open up the shot."

I take the note and plow into another stuntman, leading with my shoulder before wrapping my opposite arm around his trunk and pulling. We fall to the mat beneath us.

"Cut! That was much better, thank you. Colt, places!"

He takes his spot next to me. This is the first time we're running a scene side by side, with one camera trained on Colt to capture up-close frames and another pulling wide to cover the fighting happening between Ares—me—and Odysseus, on behalf of Athena.

While we wait for Francesca to roll camera, Colt tells me my work looks sharp.

Then he catches my eye. "Did you see the girls earlier?" He means Ana and her double, who were also filming side-by-sides this morning. And I did—it was a masterclass in working together to capture the exact emotional and physical mood Francesca wanted for the scene. She seemed thrilled by how it was turning out in real time. I was mesmerized watching Ana in her element. Powerful, intentional.

When each scene cut, she rallied the troops, grabbing bottles of water for her castmates from craft services and shouting words of encouragement. She was also quick to throw an arm around my waist and lean her head against my shoulder when she found me there watching her. It felt good to tuck her against me for a moment, to kiss the top of her head, before sending her back. It seemed like every eye in the place was on us, or every eye but Colt's.

"Oh, yeah. They did a great job," I tell him, stretching out my lower back, stiff from all the crouching.

"Better than I expected," Colt says. "I've never thought Ana was right for this role. Between you and me, I pushed to get her replaced."

*Pushed to get her replaced.* "Yeah, that *Hollywood Star* rumor must have been . . . not great for you," I say.

"No, before that."

I start to ask him what he means when we hear, "Roll camera!" and it's too late.

The day we met, Ana told me that Francesca was considering recasting her role to prevent more negative press. But Colt *trying* to get Ana fired, wanting her gone? That feels different. As Colt slips back into character, he clears his throat, like what he said was casual, but unease drips through me. His words sit in my stomach, loaded and leaden.

When Francesca yells action, I channel every bit of my building discomfort into the poor guy working opposite me. My mind is a threshing drum trying to sort through my thoughts.

*Maybe it's ultimately the same thing, what he said versus what Ana told me.*

*Would I want to know if a coworker—not the director, but a peer—tried to undercut my career?*

*It's possible Ana already knows this about Colt. She probably does. Maybe it doesn't matter.*

*But what if she doesn't know? Should I tell her?*

*If I do, she might go to Francesca to talk about it. It may get back to Colt.*

*I'd look like a snake. He could convince Francesca to choose someone else for the next film.*

*Maybe I'm overthinking the whole thing.*

*What a shitty fucking thing for him to do to her.*

The thought of Colt trying to mess with Ana's job flares in my chest, and the white-hot frustration comes out through my fists. It's not until Francesca yells, "Cut, Levi. Cut. CUT!" that I realize the scene ended and I'm still slamming this poor guy into the floor.

"Shit, sorry! Sorry."

Francesca raises her hands like she wants to shake me. "Go take a beat."

When my anger finally burns off, what's left is embarrassment. That, and awareness of something I can't ignore: I feel protective of her. Whether or not I should.

The internal warning system I expect to go off, the one that should be telling me to slow down, instead says, *Is it really so bad?* It's not bad to want the best for someone, a friend or a coworker.

*Focus on what you can control.* The phrase comes to mind in my dad's voice, nagging and unwelcome. He must've said it, and I must've heard it, fifteen thousand times growing up. Though it kills me to admit—and I would never, not to him—it's solid advice. I can't control what happens if I share Colt's remark. How Ana would respond. How Colt would react. I *can* control doing excellent work on this film and showing up with Ana, both things I agreed to. I can double down on what's working and keep my attention there.

That feels safe for both Ana and me.

Though, if I'm honest, my feelings are starting to feel less safe by the day.

Three raps on Ana's trailer door turn into eight before I finally hear a "Yeah?"

"Hey, it's me—can I come in?"

She opens it up an inch, enough to peek an eye and one side of her face through. "I'm not dressed yet."

"Even better." I wink, and she knows it's a joke—of course, it's a joke—but the way she flushes isn't.

"What I mean is I'm not in my next costume yet. I'm not naked, I have a robe on."

"Perfect. Open up."

She swings the door wide and sucks in a breath as I glide up the stairs and into her trailer. "OK, *you're* naked."

I'm not—I'm in costume, but the scene requires more, in the words of the wardrobe department, "glistening skin" than actual garments. Bare chest. A lot of quad. I clear my throat. "Oh, yeah, sorry, we're about to reset, but I thought you . . ." I stop before I say, *should know what Colt said*. Because, no, dumbass. That's not what I should say. I'm focusing on what I can control. Instead, I manage, "I thought you'd like this idea I had." I'm fumbling, but she doesn't seem to notice.

This is the first time we've been alone on set since filming started. It feels at least ten degrees warmer inside this trailer than it did outside. She crosses her arms over her chest before looking me up and down. "Actually, I have an idea for you too."

"Oh yeah?" This is good, because my idea? I still need to come up with one.

"The photos of us kissing took off. Should we stage one in here? People love a BTS."

"The . . . boyband?"

She raps a hand against my abs. "No, Farmer Jim, behind the scenes. B-T-S."

"Farmer Jim? Really?"

"If the muck boots fit . . ." I notice the twist of her lips and the laugh caught in her throat.

"And what do *you* know about muck?" I reach over and toy with the soft terrycloth belt of her robe. It makes it too easy to tug her closer to me, and she comes willingly.

"Just that that's where we'll be stuck if people start to doubt that we're dating. Are you in?"

"Whatever you want," I answer, because I don't trust myself to say yes without sounding overeager. Of course the answer is yes. I've been thinking about our kisses at the hospital, and the contented *hmm* that came from her throat, for days now.

She pulls me over to her couch and yanks me down to sit next to her. She positions her phone in the center of a stand with a ring light. Adjusting the height to capture us on the couch, she flips to the front camera and scoots left on the cushions with a tug for me to follow. "How's this?" She gestures to the two of us on the screen.

I laugh. "It's a lot of my abs."

"That's half the point. We'll do a video. I'll grab a still." She leans forward to press record, and I realize we should've made a game plan, because now we're just looking at each other. I can't stand the silence, and I hear myself say, "Game on," as I bring a hand to her jaw and lean in. I miss the chance to regret the words because her eyes flutter closed, her hand grips my forearm, and she brings her mouth to mine.

She starts with one, two, three light presses of her lips. I can see us frame by frame in my mind, and it looks like a stage kiss. It *feels* like a stage kiss. I move my hand to the back of her head and grip. "I know you can do better than that," I whisper into her mouth. She leans away to catch my gaze, to watch my expression as she drops her hand from my arm and glides it up my thigh. She doesn't wait for me to respond before diving back into the kiss and pulling my bottom lip between hers.

The sudden pressure of her fingertips and the hot slide of her tongue against mine is more than I meant but exactly what I need. My fingers thread through her hair and pull; my groan fills the space where her breath catches. When she walks her hand over my hip to the exposed flesh of my stomach and runs her fingernails along the skin, my control snaps. I bring a hand to her chest and push to lay her down, chasing her mouth as I hover over her. She tightens an arm around my neck to keep me there.

*Buzz.*

The vibration of the text message feels as startling as a gong. Ana gasps and pulls back her arm; I sit up and shake out my shoulders. She scrambles to her feet and reties the belt of her robe before reaching for her phone.

"I guess we were out of frame for some of that," I say. It's stupid. She doesn't want to talk about how *not fake* the moment became.

"Yeah. Pretty, uh, convincing though." She takes a deep breath. "Good work."

I run a hand through my hair. "You too."

Awkwardness hangs in the air like fog. We're back to staring at each other with no plan forward. It's then I remember that I'm supposed to have a scheme myself.

"So um. My idea," I start, and something thankfully materializes. "Since we're off tomorrow and I need groceries—maybe you could come with me."

". . . To the store?" Her raised eyebrow says no but I continue anyway.

"Yeah. It'll be fun. A normal couple activity, like a casual date."

"Getting coffee is a casual date. Getting groceries is a chore. At best, an errand."

I lean against a shallow counter and cross one ankle in front of the other. "An opportunity to show people we're happy together, even doing something mundane."

One side of her bottom lip is pulled between her teeth as she considers the idea. I keep my eyes on hers. She fiddles again with the belt of her robe.

"OK," she agrees with a nod. I try to keep my grin from spreading too wide.

As I walk toward the trailer door, I tell her I'll text her

about logistics. I hop down the stairs, stop at the bottom, and turn back. "And Ana?"

"Yeah?" She's leaning against the doorframe and peering down at me. She meets my eyes, and her face brightens.

"Anything can be a date with the right intentions."

**Instagram**

**@anabarlow** Happy.

**@ashley_robb** WOW WOW WOW yes girl get it!! 🔥

**@erika17warren** I thought this was Colt for a second **@annie.warren**

**@annie.warren** LMFAO

**@starbucksandstardust** Colt isn't trashy enough to post something like this

**@heykellyhey** I didn't know a 12 pack was a thing

**@tiptops10** what exactly did you pray for **@anabarlow**

**@gemma_kt** 👏 I need THE EXACT WORDS

**@tampabayby** Oh you are RICH rich

**@andy699669** is he available for weddings? Like as the groom? I'm married but we aren't that serious

**@healthnut148** happy for you, he seems nice

**@allie_ccccat** this bitch is back on her bullshit for attention 💀 **@jojonewton**

**@jojonewton** she's got mine BARK BARK

**@trish.john.murphy** no one cares **@anabarlow**

*Load 1,289 additional comments*

# XII

## ANA

"Em, what do people in Nashville wear to go grocery shopping?" I'm shouting from inside the closet in my rental—a four-bedroom in Williamson County with a three-way mirror in the walk-in wardrobe. I've never set foot in a Publix, and I have to imagine it's a different vibe from Erewhon—different energies for different grocery allegiances. We're two weeks into filming here, but I haven't gotten out enough to have a sense of what's normal attire in this town.

Emily leans against the doorframe with her arms crossed over her chest. "Are you asking me for outfit advice so you can blend in with us common folk?" Smug. That's the look on her face right now as I flip through the hangers: smug.

"Are you going to help me, or should I google it? I need something easy, cute."

"Cute because this is an opportunity to get people

talking, or cute because you're seeing Levi off set?" She smacks her lips to accompany the question.

"Yes—both—does it matter?"

"You tell me. The picture of you two kissing in your trailer had *me* convinced you're basically in love with the guy, and I was there when you came up with this sham relationship."

Her words make the skin on my chest warm, a sure indication that, under my T-shirt, I'm turning red. After ten years of climbing the ladder together, letting her role in my life evolve from manager to manager–slash–best friend, I should know better than to try to get anything past her. But I don't want to let on that she might be right. I'm not even sure how to read what she's seeing myself.

"I'm an actress, Emily." I rustle through dresses to avoid eye contact. "Did you think I'd fake a relationship and not throw myself into it? Making it look real is the whole point."

"So you're *not* trying to impress Levi with a 'Look at me, I'm so down-to-earth' grocery store outfit?" Of course, she has me pegged. I keep my eyes trained on the wall of clothes. "Because if you're not, go with leggings and a big button-down." She picks up a pair of black Tom Ford leggings and tosses them my way. I catch them before immediately lobbing them back at her.

"OK, maybe I am. Trying to impress him. Happy? It's just been—he's not what I expected." That's an understatement. He's the opposite of what I expected. I assumed he'd be one of those guys who offers muscles in place of a personality like that's a meaningful trade. But he's witty and considerate and always seems to know what I need. He isn't afraid of me. And most importantly, he seems to view me as a person—not an asset. I shrug and hope Emily doesn't notice the blush that I catch creeping up my neck in the mirrors.

She pumps a fist twice in the air. "Ha! I knew it. You like him."

I roll my eyes. What is this, middle school? "Of course, I like him. He's incredibly likable. But you and I both know getting involved for real is a bad idea. I can't risk this falling apart while we're filming. I can't risk anything interfering with what this role could be for me."

It doesn't matter how much I like him, and like kissing him. That's just an added perk, and I should take it for what it is.

"I think that's smart. Eyes on the prize and all that." She points two fingers at her face and then mine.

"Great, now help me figure out what to wear."

"Fresh mozzarella or shredded?" Levi holds one in each hand like Lady Justice weighing the scales.

"Fresh. Obviously." I grab the ball of cheese and place it in my basket. "If you're making pizza at home, you might as well make it better than a frozen one."

He returns the shredded cheese and tucks a hand into the pocket of his fitted dark jeans, just under the hem of his white Henley. It shows off his tan, making his skin look as warm as I know it is. It's cold in the dairy section, and I wouldn't mind feeling it against me.

He chooses this moment to drape an arm around my shoulders, his large, rough hand radiating heat where his fingers press into my skin below the sleeve of the fitted floral top Em recommended.

"Any other feedback?" he replies with a wink. The flutter of his lashes prompts a flutter in my stomach.

"You'll need dough." We continue down the refrigerated aisle spanning the store's back wall. Levi chuckles and grips my arm tighter. "Shoot, there was a 'knead dough' pun in there, and I missed it, huh?" I look over at him.

"There's still thyme." He grabs a small box of the herb and tosses it into the basket. "You might say it's not *thyme sensitive*." He laughs at his own joke, and I can't help but join him. The giggle tickles in my chest with the warmth and fizz of expensive champagne. God, I didn't know how much I needed this: something easy and *fun* in my life.

"Basil, you dork. We need basil. Thyme doesn't belong anywhere near a pizza." I whack him playfully on the stomach, relishing the firm response of his abs as the back of my hand makes contact. He swaps the herbs, and we dodge a few other shoppers as we turn into the canned foods aisle. "Have you always had a love affair with pizza, or was this just the easiest thing to shop for on an exceedingly domestic grocery store date?" I ask.

"Is there a person alive who doesn't like pizza? Of course, I love pizza. And where else are you going to get all five food groups in one dish? Grains, dairy, protein, veggies, fruit . . ."

"You are *not* putting pineapple on this pizza, Levi." I try to shoot him a side-eye, but a smile sneaks through.

"Hey, if you'll remember, this is *my* dinner. You're here to help me shop. What I do with the ingredients later is none of your business." With that, he sneaks his hand under mine and steals the shopping basket for himself. Mischief is written all over his face, in the glint of his eyes and the lines above his raised brows.

"What if I want to join you for dinner? Then could we skip the pineapple?"

"Are you inviting yourself over, Barlow?" He cocks his head to the side, appraising me.

"Are you saying I can't come?"

"I'd never deny a lady who's eager to come." He says it with a grin so wide the small dimple appears on his cheek.

I have to avert my eyes so he can't see the way they spark at the innuendo. "Wow, OK, at least your bad produce pun was *appropriate*."

He smirks. "Of course you're welcome to join. We can post about it. What else should we get, now that we're extending this date?"

Tucking me tighter to his side, he drops a kiss to the top

of my head. Just like a boyfriend. I wrap my arm around his waist and revel in the soft exhale that escapes him when I slip my fingertips under the hem of his shirt to graze his skin. Just like a girlfriend. Behind us, the wheels of a cart squeak against the linoleum.

"What we have is fine. I had a big lunch, so I probably won't eat much anyway."

Levi stops abruptly, nearly causing a collision with the older woman cruising just behind us. She veers to our right with a scowl. He locks his eyes on mine. "Eating lunch doesn't mean you skip dinner."

The attention makes me squirm—hits me with a desire to step out of my skin and replace my soul with the cardboard cutout version that shows up on red carpets and interviews. The manufactured "me" that everyone's words and expectations slide right off of, that doesn't have a soft spot, tender and exposed, beneath her ribs.

My walls want to go up, but Levi's stare holds them down. He *sees* me, and he's begging to be let in.

"It's . . ." I stall, then move us into the next empty aisle. This isn't a conversation I want replayed on TikTok later. "My relationship with food is a work in progress. The camera adds ten pounds, stylists want me to lose twenty. Hollywood rewards smallness, you know?" I scan his form. "Well, for women. And when I look in the mirror, it's like my lens is warped. I'm better now than I used to be—I try to eat when I'm hungry, think of food as fuel, all that—but when something big comes around . . ."

"Big like *Athena's War*?" he asks, and I can't believe we're talking about this in the spice aisle of a Tennessee Publix. Levi has this way of shepherding me between playfully silly and starkly vulnerable with a level of assuredness that makes me feel safe. It's as freeing as it is unnerving. It's something no one else has ever been able to do—or, perhaps, something I've never let anyone else do. What that means, I'm not sure I'm ready to interrogate.

"Yes, like *Athena's War*."

We turn toward the row of cashiers, and there we are, in a photo climbing into Edwin's car in the top-right corner of *Celebs Weekly* magazine, "Who Is Levi Stephens?" printed underneath. The tabloid is one of many on the shelf, each with a feature of us somewhere on the cover. We're not the biggest story—we're buried well under "Jack Felgate, Sexiest Man Alive"—but we're there.

Levi drops his arm from around me to weave his fingers through mine. "If it helps, I have my own hang-ups. I was the scrawny kid growing up. Too tall, knock-kneed, with more ribs than abs. I was a bottomless pit for years, and my mom always joked I had a hollow leg—where else was all the food going?"

I chance a look at his face, and his eyes are soft. Reminiscing. I wonder what it must be like to think of your childhood, your family, with any measure of fondness. He doesn't know what a gift it is.

He points to the endcap as we approach the registers. "Seeing these photos, plus the social media comments talking about how ripped I am . . . it's hard to reconcile. In my head, I'm still a hundred and forty pounds soaking wet, trying to be taken seriously and working my ass off to bulk up. I don't think I see myself clearly either."

He grips my hand, pulls me with him to a self-checkout station, and doesn't let go as he scans our items.

Did someone take our picture through the large glass windows at the front of the store? I'm not sure. But if the goal was to make it look like our connection is deepening, we definitely nailed it.

# XIII

## LEVI

This rental apartment where I'm staying can't be what Ana is used to. It's a one-bedroom in a complex close to set that's filled with other members of the cast and crew who weren't afforded the star treatment. I'm keenly aware of its size as Ana pokes around the kitchen, looking for a baking sheet.

She opens a cabinet and unearths a silicone brush. "I'm impressed by the number of kitchen tools in this place. Have you been cooking a lot?"

"Not once since we got here." I lean against the smooth granite counter and watch her squat to pull out the drawer under the oven. The movement makes her low-slung jeans pull tight across her hips and ass. I should look away, but I can't seem to find the will. Ana may have trouble appreciating her body, but I don't. Soft curves leading to the cut of her waist, the dip of her shirt revealing her collarbone. Wavy blonde hair falls behind her shoulders, and I'd like to brush it away to expose the spot just behind her ear. To kiss her there and watch her shiver.

"Got it!" Ana holds the sheet pan above her head, victorious.

"To be honest, I wasn't sure you'd find one." I have to work hard to pull my thoughts back to the pizza.

"Start slicing the mozzarella, and I'll stretch the dough." She points a finger at me and then to the ball of cheese on the counter, and I can't help but smile. I told her the day we met that "blonde and demanding" wasn't my type, but I'll be damned if that hasn't changed. That she knows what she wants and is willing to ask for it—it's working for me in a way I didn't expect.

I circle the counter, heading toward a knife block on the other side, but there's no way to squeeze by her without pressing either my ass or crotch to her body.

I consider my options and take a step toward her, placing one hand on the counter. Cold from the stone surface seeps into my palm. "Sorry, I'm just gonna squeeze past you," I whisper, tipping my mouth to her ear before bringing my other arm to her other side, effectively caging her in from behind. "Not a lot of room here."

It may be my imagination—or some unacknowledged hope—but I swear she leans back a touch, settling her back against my chest, relaxing into this posture that was meant to be momentary.

My heart rate spikes, and I forget myself. "I've never used fresh dough. Show me?" I completely abandon my purpose for stepping behind her and cling to a reason to stay here.

Her ass grazes the tops of my thighs as she turns her face to look up at me, and I hold my breath as she narrows her eyes. Sussing me out, like she still can't decide if there's something untrustworthy beneath my words. I nod toward the dough.

"It wants to retain its shape." She leans forward, palming the sticky ball on the sheet in front of her. "You stretch it, and it pulls back, resisting. It takes a lot of patience and persistence to get it where you want it. For it to expand. To where it'll stay." Ana looks at me then, and the wariness from a moment before is gone. Instead, there's something seeking, something pressing in her eyes that makes me wonder if she's not just talking about pizza crust. Like she might want to take a new shape too, if only someone would hold her when she wants to shrink back.

"Like this?" I place my hand over hers, and suddenly we're cosplaying *Ghost*. It should feel awkward, but it doesn't. It feels good to be close to her. It feels right to have her in my space. It feels natural to touch her, even when there are no cameras around to catch it. Based on how her breathing's picked up, I think the feeling's mutual. What this means in the grand scheme of our ruse—or outside of it—I'm not sure.

"Yes, just like that." She nods before bringing her hand, and mine with it, back to the center of the tray.

"Do you want me to take over while you cut the cheese?" A giggle bursts out of her at my unintentional potty humor—my mouth moving faster than my brain again—and her body heaves against mine like this need to let go of herself was lingering just below the surface. The bright, shrill pitch of her laugh catches like a hook in my chest, pulling my own laughter from somewhere deep in me with enough force to ruffle her hair. She struggles to catch her breath. Temptation wins, and I bring my mouth to her throat, to that spot just behind her jaw, below her ear.

"You," I whisper, before dotting a kiss there, "might be," I press another, "the most intriguing person," and another, "I've ever met."

Ana pushes the tray away before turning in my arms to face me. I lift her to sit on the counter, her legs dangling between mine.

"Well, you," she says, looping her arms behind my neck, "might be the only one special enough to see it."

I close the remaining distance between us and bring my hips flush against hers. Something is happening here. The air is thick with it—anticipation, curiosity, all the caution we both seem to be throwing to the wind. I expect her to pull away, to remind me, or herself, that this isn't something we're supposed to do.

But she doesn't. She wraps her legs around my waist, so I hover my mouth over hers, with just a breath of space between her lips and mine. While I wait—to see if she'll lean forward or if I'll have the courage to close the gap myself—I pluck at my last thread of reason. If we kiss, it'll make our chemistry more believable in public. If we kiss, maybe this desire that's starting to boil in my chest will slow to a simmer. Maybe it'll be easier to control. The thread snaps. "Can I kiss you?" I ask.

Her "yes" comes out like a prayer as I settle my mouth on hers. *There's less pressure without the cameras.* Or is there more pressure without the cameras?

I bring a hand to cradle her jaw and angle her face for a deeper kiss. She parts my mouth with her tongue, and a groan echoes from my lungs as we settle into a rhythm—pushing and pulling, giving and taking, asking and responding. As she rakes a hand through my hair, she keeps her mouth tight to mine, breaking only to run her lips over the length of my jaw, to bite softly on my earlobe before soothing it with a soft suck.

Then it's tangled tongues, sighs, and the grip of her teeth on my bottom lip. Wandering fingertips and stroking skin, the front of my jeans growing tighter when she whimpers under my touch. It's new and familiar, comfortable and maybe the scariest thing I've ever done, kissing her like this.

It's not fake.

It's *easy.*

After a minute, maybe ten, Ana pulls her lips from my neck with a quiet pop and leans back on her hands to catch my gaze. Her cheeks are pink, her hair is mussed, and she's glowing. Absolutely, overwhelmingly beautiful.

"I promised I was going to feed you dinner," I say,

forcing my focus back to the kitchen. We glance at the half-prepped pizza dough behind her. She reaches to her left and plucks a knife from the block.

"Then start slicing the mozzarella, Levi. If you stay on my side of the kitchen, I can't promise we'll get to the food. The rest of this," she circles her finger between us, "can wait."

I steal one more quick kiss before asking, "And what is it we're doing here? What is *this*?"

"Hmmm." She bites her cheek. "I think we're playing house." She sets down the knife and brings her hands to mine. I nod. I see what she's doing here. She knows as well as I do that we're not playing, but sure, I can tag along with the lie.

A breath blows out of me as I peel myself from between her legs, my fingers lingering on her thighs until the last possible moment. I grab the cheese and unwrap it, never breaking eye contact with her as I do. "Then I'll get to slicing."

"You were right about the fresh mozzarella," I say to Ana, who's finishing a slice of pizza while sitting on the other end of the couch, her legs draped over mine.

She smiles and wags her brows. "I'm always right."

I grip her foot in one hand and run my thumb along the sole, tickling until she pulls away with a shriek.

"You're gonna pay for that." She sets her plate on the coffee table and bends forward to sink a hand to the top of my thigh, just above my knee. She squeezes, and I try not to react, but the grin twitching at my lips begs to be set free.

"Don't start something you can't finish, Barlow." I steal her hand from my leg and wrap it in my palm. She shifts closer to me and lays her head on my shoulder. A wave of coconut from her hair mingles with the scent of freshly baked dough, and I know it's a smell I'll be nostalgic about for the rest of my life.

"Thank you for this," she says with a contented sigh. Its effect is like a weighted blanket, calming my mind, which has been bouncing back and forth about whether we're crossing a line we shouldn't.

She curls her legs under her. "For today. Tonight. It's not often that I get to do 'normal' stuff like this. I'm starting to realize how rare it is that I can actually relax." She runs her thumb over my hand, an absentminded touch. "Promise me you won't get a big head, but it's been nice to spend time with you. To know I can trust you, that I don't have to worry you'll turn around and sell my secrets tomorrow."

"I won't." My words are decisive, firm. But the phrase "I can trust you" twists in my stomach. *I tried to get her replaced.* Colt's words ping-pong around my head. Do I want to ruin this, her rare moment of peace, to ask her about it? Do I want to risk it getting back to Colt somehow?

My phone buzzes with an incoming call. It's Edwin.

He must be outside to take Ana home.

"Hey, man," I answer, bringing my right hand around Ana's shoulder to trace along her arm as I keep her tucked to my side.

"Glad I got ahold of you. Have you seen the alert?" he asks.

"No?" I start racing through the possibilities.

"There's a tornado watch, and it's heading toward a warning. The agency has halted all activity for the night, so I can't get there to take Ana home. Check the weather—y'all should think about staying put until it blows through."

That is not at all what I expected out of this call. "OK. Hmmm. Yeah, OK." I give myself a few moments to think. "We'll hang here. I'll touch base with you in the morning."

He ends the call, and I let the phone drop to my lap. Tornado warnings aren't new to me; Ohio gets them too. We have *basements* in Ohio, though.

"So, change of plans," I say, turning to her. "You're staying here tonight."

# XIV

## ANA

"I'm doing what, now?" No toothbrush, no deodorant, no change of clothes—this isn't happening.

"There's a tornado watch. Edwin isn't coming."

"What is this, Kansas? We're in a major city. That can't be right." I grab my phone and search for "Nashville" and "tornado." And there it is, the top result, about Tennessee being the country's leader in nocturnal tornadoes. What the fuck.

I look up to see Levi run a hand down his face, looking worried and a little bit hurt. My stomach drops. He thinks I can't fathom spending the night with him. I acted like this was the worst possible outcome. This wasn't the plan, but we can make it work. A little . . . spontaneous sleepover. Between coworkers. Who already kissed today, off camera. Kissed in a way that has me oscillating between a panicked mental state of *What the hell are we doing right now?* and a horny physical state of *If he feels it too, then why not have fun?*

If I spend the night here, I'm not entirely sure which one will win out.

"Hey, it's fine," I say, shifting my body toward him and trying to change the energy in the room. "You know what we'll do? We'll keep doing what we're doing. We'll sit on the couch and eat more pizza and you'll say something cheesy to make me laugh and I'll share something I might regret. It'll be a classic sleepover. Nothing but fun."

Levi's pupils widen, and he pulls his lips to the side, pinching the inside of his cheek between his teeth. Something about the expression sends a zip of electricity down my spine. It's timid, almost. *Is he nervous?*

"A sleepover . . ." He draws out the word. "Yeah. That'll be fine. You can have the bed, and I'll take the couch."

"Are you suggesting you could comfortably curl up on what is actually a loveseat?" I point to the piece of furniture beneath us, just two leather cushions wide with curved armrests on each end.

He squints, as if he's trying to envision how he'd tuck in his limbs. "I could do it."

"No, you're not going to do that. And with my joints, I'm not subjecting myself to this either. We're adults, we can share the bed. Like I said, it'll be fine."

"OK." He nods, trying and failing to sound casual.

"Great. Settled." I will myself to believe that it *will* be great. "But you need to find me something to wear. I'm not staying in these jeans for the next however many hours."

I place my hands on his shoulders and push him to stand before nudging him toward a door I'm assuming is the bedroom. He disappears behind it, and I allow myself a big breath, then attempt to push out the nerves brewing in my stomach along with the air.

"Are you sure you're ready for this?" I peek out at him from the cracked-open door of the bathroom, absolutely drowning in one of Levi's workout tanks. It's paired with basketball shorts that hang like a midi skirt, even though I rolled them up four times. This is not the sexy, I-dare-you-to-keep-your-hands-off-me outfit I usually wear when spending the night with someone for the first time. This is giving Adam Sandler. I look *ridiculous.*

"Couldn't be more ready."

But the moment I emerge from the bathroom, like a beautiful butterfly who managed to reverse engineer herself back into a caterpillar, his mouth drops open.

"Geez, I know it's bad, but I didn't expect speechless-level bad."

"Nope, that's, ah, not what's happening here." He squirms in his seat. "I've got a beautiful woman in front of me wearing my clothes. I'm gonna need a minute." A flush reddens the tips of his ears.

He watches from the couch as I make my way to him, a

glint in his eyes that sears heat into my chest. I don't miss how his gaze lingers on my sides, how the wide holes of his tank expose the black lace of my bra underneath.

He reaches out and grabs me around the waist, his arms enveloping my body. "Get over here." I fall into him, and we're immediately a mess of tangled limbs and laughter. The couch cushions squeak beneath us.

When we settle, resuming our positions from earlier with my legs draped over his lap, I watch his eyes travel the length of my body. When he reaches a bloom of blue and purple on my shin, his attention snags, and he sucks in a breath.

"What'd you do here?" He traces the outline of the bruise with a whisper of a touch, an attempt to comfort without pressing on the tender skin. The gentleness of his fingertips, the care in his voice—it catches me off guard. This version of him is so soft. It's not what I'm used to with men. It would be dangerous to get used to it.

"Funny enough, I'm not sure how I got that." I meet his gaze with a half-smile and a shrug, trying to convey a levity I don't quite feel. His eyebrows raise and his head cocks to the side, unconvinced. "Unexplained bruises are pretty common for me. They're . . . well . . . they're another way my condition shows up. I tend to run into things. I spent twenty-eight years thinking I was distracted and clumsy, only to find out last year that I have issues with proprioception. Try saying that five times fast." I attempt to force out a laugh, but it comes out like a wince. Levi pulls his hand from my leg like it's a hot stove.

"Oh, no, trust me—you're fine. I'm fine. I'm trying to make sure you know this bruise isn't a big deal, and I'm clearly failing at it." I feel desperate to pull away first, to save myself from falling into the trap where I bare my faults and the person responds by retreating from my life. But his eyes stay on mine, searching, steady. He wants something. I could pretend it's my body, but my heart fears that's the least of it. Fears that he wants my honesty. He wants my vulnerability. He wants *me.*

Rubbing his lips against each other, Levi appraises me like a collector evaluating whether a piece is real. With care and diligence, as though his investment depends on what he finds. "Why do you do that? Your reality isn't a burden, Ana. You don't need to brush it off. Tell me about this proprietary-ception thing. What does it mean?"

I smile at his attempt to find the right word, his encouragement making me brave. "Proprioception. It's a person's awareness of their body in space. Most people don't have to think about it. They inherently know where their limbs are when they're moving and how much space to give themselves when they're passing by a piece of furniture, for example."

His hand finds my leg again, his fingers resuming their pattern around the starburst of purple.

"But for people like me who have floppy joints, that

awareness isn't fine-tuned. So I miscalculate and run into stuff." Glancing up, I'm caught by the earnestness in his expression, the way his pupils are blown. "The kicker, though, is that I'm more likely to bruise when I do bump into things. You know what I told you about my connective tissue? The collagen in my vessels also doesn't—"

"—doesn't keep the blood well contained," he says, completing the thought for me. The way he says this, putting the pieces together on his own without a hint of pity, builds a stinging pressure behind my eyes. He already knows more than anyone else in my life, but he seems eager for all of it. My fear loses ground to the desire to be known.

I look back down at the purple bloom and decide to risk sharing more. "Yeah. It's pretty innocuous with the bruises and hyperflexible joints, but—and I try not to think about this a lot—the vascular part can be life-threatening. I'm scheduled to see a cardiologist every three years to make sure I don't end up with a giant aneurysm like my grandfather. His artery stretched and stretched until you could see the blood pulsing in his abdomen through his shirt."

I'm lost in the memory for a moment, standing beside my grandpa's hospital bed while he charmed every nurse within a fifteen-foot radius. It makes me smile. If only I inherited his charisma along with his crap blood vessels.

Levi's warm exhale of breath pulls me back to the present, to the sight of him leaning forward, studying the bruise that's taking too much of our attention. He bends further and dots a series of soft kisses around the perimeter.

Goose bumps spring up at each spot where the heat of his mouth lingers. I can't stop myself from threading my fingers through his hair, from touching him with some measure of affection. Affection that is, admittedly, more guarded than what he's showing me.

"Is it weird if I say I like this bruise?" Glancing up to meet my gaze, his eyes crinkle at the corners. Maybe from tenderness, maybe from sheepishness. It's so endearing, I can hardly breathe. "I don't mean that I like that you're hurt, because obviously I don't. I wish you weren't. But I like that this part of you, this thing you hide that's invisible to the world but a constant in your life . . . I like that I get to see it. I like that you're letting me."

"I like it too," I hear myself saying.

*I like* you *too*, I don't say.

# XV

## LEVI

The first night in this apartment, I whined to the empty walls about having to trade my brand-new, king-size mattress in LA for this double. Now, with Ana tucked in next to me, her ass pressing against the outside of my thigh, I send up a silent prayer of gratitude for the tight fit.

"Getting comfy over there?" I adjust the blanket under my arms.

"Would you believe me if I said this bed is better than all the five-star hotels I've ever stayed in? What kind of memory-foam, pillow-top magic *is* this? You've gotta ask the management company." She rolls to face me. Relaxed. That's how she looks in this moment. Content, with hair piled into a mess on top of her head and a makeup-free face, the sweetest freckles I didn't know she had scattered across the bridge of her nose and her cheeks.

I can't help but press my lips to the constellation of them, a quick peck at one spot and then the next.

"Levi," she says between breaths. I keep going. "Levi!"

She laughs before grabbing my face with her hands and melting her lips onto mine.

On instinct, I wrap an arm around her, pressing my palm to the small of her back and guiding her closer. She throws a leg over my hip, the slippery fabric of my basketball shorts on her gliding over the slippery fabric of my basketball shorts on me. The improbability of this moment—of Ana Barlow in my bed, wearing my clothes, kissing me like she wants something—I'm overwhelmed by it.

*How in the world did I get so lucky?*

"What's that about getting lucky?" Ana pulls her lips from mine to press her mouth to my bare shoulder. I've let an inside thought slip out of my mouth—again. Before I can beat myself up about it, she's dragging her tongue along my collarbone, and I feel it like a finger tracing my length. Every bit of blood in my body rushes south. Warm, tingling anticipation.

"I said I *feel* lucky. Being here with you." I bring her mouth back to mine and let my tongue find hers. She responds with a sigh and a roll of her hips I'm not sure is intentional. We kiss leisurely, with her hands in my hair and her fingernails pressing against my scalp. I groan in response.

She has my bottom lip between her teeth as she pulls away slowly, eventually releasing it with a wet pop. "Are you saying you *don't* want to get lucky?"

Her green eyes are locked on mine, and they're darker

without sunlight to bring out the usual flecks of gold. Or maybe it's that her pupils are wide and hungry. She tilts her head with a smirk, those swollen lips of hers pulled to one side.

"I want whatever you want," I tell her. Yes, there are many things I want with her, especially after today. But what I want most of all is for her to know she's in charge. That I'm not another asshole who's here for an Ana Barlow–shaped notch in his bedpost. That I'm not like Colt, who's willing to prioritize himself at someone else's expense.

"Well, I want to lose this shirt." She shifts to her knees, and with a quick sweep of her arm, she pulls the tank over her head and flings it onto the floor.

*Want, want, want,* beats my heart in response. "You are absolutely unreal. Do you know that?" I don't hide the way I'm taking her in as I sit up and reach for her, and she doesn't try to hide from me, though I can feel a flush on her neck when my fingers make contact with her collarbone.

I catalog her.

The freckles extend to her chest, to the space above the cups of her bra, which barely contain the swell of her breasts. Her stomach is soft, kissable. A faded bruise lingers on the inside of one arm. The curled-up waistband of my shorts—those damn shorts—prevents me from following the curve of her waist to her hips.

She's watching me take her in. My heart is flying against my ribs.

With an adept flick, she releases the clasp of her bra and tosses it to the floor. "How about now? Even better?"

I move my hands toward her waist, and she collapses on top of me, bracing herself on her arms to hold her lips a hair's breadth from mine. Her hard nipples brush against my chest. "The best." I crash my mouth into hers for a moment before flipping us so I'm on top.

"Now that smooth move—the scoop and flip you just did? That's gotta be from stunt school." A smile curls her lips.

"Maybe. Or maybe it's something I improvised because I couldn't wait another second to get my mouth on you." I suck on her neck before slowly bringing my lips to her chest. She arches toward me with a moan. My tongue finds her nipple, pink and peaked, and I close my mouth around it, flicking slowly. "I'm going to take my time with you," I tell her between passes of my tongue.

I bring my hand to her opposite breast. I pinch the nipple between my fingers, and she squirms under my touch. "Is this where you want me?" She nods, like it's all she can do. Her breast is full, and I palm it, pressing my fingertips into her flesh before dragging them down her side. I stop at the waistband of the shorts, which have slipped to expose an inch of black lace. "Or here?" I run a finger beneath the top seam of her underwear, her warm, bare skin dragging under mine.

"Take them off." It comes out of her mouth breathy, begging as much as demanding. I feel it behind my ribs, in the dryness of my mouth, in my cock. She shimmies her hips and hooks a thumb under the elastic to assist.

"Ana." I press a hand over hers to stop her. "I said I'm taking my time. Let me."

I sit back on my heels and dig my fingers under both waistbands. Without removing my eyes from hers, I peel away her shorts and underwear and then stand to take off my own.

"How's this? Better?" I echo her words from earlier, and she replies with a laugh and an eye roll before grabbing my arms and pulling me back down on top of her. My cock twitches with the press of her bare stomach against me.

"The best."

I sink my mouth onto hers for a moment before kissing her sternum, then bringing my lips back to her nipple. I can't help my smile at the sound of her sharp intake of breath when I give it a gentle bite.

"Where do you want me to touch you?" I place my fingers at her jaw, and then trail them down her body, pausing in spots where I notice her breath hitches: her throat, her breast, her stomach.

"Levi, please." She cants her hips toward me.

"Please, what?" I lift my head to meet her gaze.

"You know what."

"Sweetheart, I need to hear you say it." I draw my hand down her abdomen until the heavy weight of it lies just above her pubic bone. She moans at the pressure.

"Touch me. I want to feel your fingers inside of me," she whispers.

Whatever conviction I had to take this slow evaporates. My hand slips down to cup her, to part her with my thumb, to dip inside of her—wet and warm—with one finger and then another. I bring my mouth to hers and feel her stuttering breaths on my lips between kisses.

"God, that feels good," she says, and I slide the pad of my finger, slick with her, to her clit. I trace circles that echo the rhythm of our mouths, and the way she whimpers when I slip back inside her—I could run a marathon with nothing but her noises for fuel. Soft, pleading noises, until she says my name.

"Levi. I swear, you're going to make me come."

A laugh tries to escape my mouth, but she stifles it with another kiss, gripping the hair at the nape of my neck. "That's the plan, sweetheart. What do you need?" I stroke her, increasing the speed of my fingers to mirror the rate of her breaths.

"Just . . . like that. Yes. Oh my God, keep doing that."

I glide wetness from inside her up to where she's most sensitive, circling, pressing, stroking until I feel her legs begin to tremble beneath me.

"That's it," I say, pressed to her mouth. "You're so good. You're going to let me see you come, aren't you? You're going to be so beautiful when you fall apart."

She moans against my lips as the release overtakes her,

eyes fluttering shut and tiny spasms squeezing my hand at her center.

"Good girl, I've got you." I wrap both arms around her and pull us to our sides, nose-to-nose, heaving breaths echoing between us. I press my palm against her lower back to steady us.

"Levi?" Her eyes pop open and search mine. Vulnerable, sated, beautiful. Something else there too, but I can't put my finger on it.

"Yeah?" I bring a hand to her face and tuck a strand of hair behind her ear.

"I swear to God, if you don't have a condom in this place, I'll never forgive you." She reaches down, running her fingers along my shaft before giving a firm tug, and then another. Her expression changes with my groan, with the way my eyelids go heavy. One eyebrow lifts in question, her lower lip pulls between her teeth.

"Lucky for both of us, I do." Somehow I find the strength to hoist myself off the bed. "Don't move."

# XVI

## ANA

As Levi walks to the bathroom, I take in the view. Muscular thighs, defined back, tight ass for me to ogle. The knot of desire in my core starts to tighten again.

*"Don't move,"* I whisper to myself with a laugh. As if I could—he turned me boneless two minutes ago with just his fingers and his words. Sweet, supportive Levi has a dirty mouth, and I, apparently, have a praise kink.

He shuts the door behind him before sauntering over to the bed as though he has all the time in the world. As though his dick isn't rock hard, and I'm not wet from the sight of it.

He stops short before crawling onto the mattress. "Just want to take a mental picture of you sprawled out on this bed before we make a mess of it," he says with a smirk.

I push up on my hands, sticking out my chest and twisting my hips to give my best pin-up girl impression. Letting someone look at me like this is new. Though I'm plenty aware of my imperfections—my stretch marks and my cellulite—I can't be bothered to care when Levi's eyes fall to my tits and I watch his hand, holding the condom, twitch.

"Show's over, get over here." I rise to my knees and stretch to wrap an arm around his neck, pulling his mouth to mine. There's no more trepidation in this kiss, no more quiet sighs or waiting for a signal to take things further. Almost instantly, his hands are on my waist, his tongue is in my mouth, and his cock is pressed against my stomach. I run my fingernails down his body and then lift the weight of him in my palm, rubbing my thumb over the tip to spread his arousal. Heat grows between my legs as I stroke him. "I want you sitting up." I run my hand across the sheets.

He nods before wrapping my legs around his waist and bringing both of us to the top of the bed, his back against the headboard. "I want whatever you want."

At this moment, I think Levi Stephens would let me do just about anything to him and then ask for more. I pluck the condom from his hand, tear open the foil, and place the rubber over his tip. Slowly, carefully, I roll it down his shaft. The groan he releases washes over me like late afternoon sunshine.

I tilt forward, and with a quick press of my mouth to his, I line myself up with his length. He lifts his hips to push inside, but instead I slide back, grinding myself on his cock, over and over, until it's slick. Levi grips my hips, his fingertips pressing into the flesh to still me.

"If you're not careful, this is going to be over before it starts, sweetheart."

"You can handle it." I hold his gaze as I drag myself, slow and torturous, along his shaft.

"Ana, I swear." He holds me with bruising pressure, forgetting himself, and I wonder if I'll have marks from his fingertips tomorrow. Probably should stop my taunting.

I bring my mouth to suck on his neck, to the soft spot above his collarbone, as I notch his tip at my entrance. I lower myself slowly, taking the first inch of him on an exhale.

"Better?" I slide down another inch as his eyelids fall and his gaze goes unfocused.

"The best." His hips shift up to push deeper. A jolt of pain meets the movement.

"Wait, I just need a second to adjust." I take another deep breath and beg my pelvic floor to relax. Please.

*Please.*

"Hypertonic" is what they called it when I got my diagnosis. Tight, stiff muscles that try to compensate for the instability in my joints, even in my pelvis. Tight, stiff muscles that are sometimes—at the worst times—resistant to movement.

"I'm sorry, just . . . one more second." A witch's brew of anxiety, embarrassment, and frustration fills my chest.

"We don't have to do this." He reaches for my face and holds my jaw with both hands.

"But I want to." I'm borderline petulant, imploring him with my eyes to give me time, not to decide for me that I'm too fragile or damaged for this.

"What do you need? How can I help?"

"Keep your hand here."

I place my hand over his, bring it to my center, and lead him in slow, consistent strokes of my clit, still sensitive from before. I close my eyes. I try to focus on the movement of his thumb. I let the pleasure and pressure build. I visualize myself soft and open, and I try, with everything in me, not to worry if he's wondering what the hell is going on with me right now.

"Thank you," I say.

My eyes are still closed. His hand is still moving. And after a few too many minutes, I feel myself sink farther down his length. We both gasp at the sudden bliss of it, and I crash my mouth into his. "Thank you," I repeat between kisses. "Thank you." Again and again.

I lift myself up and down, reveling in the stretch and the way he feels inside of me and under my fingertips—the short stubble on his cheeks, the soft skin of his neck, the hard planes of his chest. It's overwhelming in the best way, and it pushes me closer to the edge.

"Ana, this is . . . shit, you feel so good."

"*You* feel so good." The movement of his fingers on me picks up speed to match our rhythm, and a moment later

I come again. Like a wave crashing, I'm hit with the full weight of my pleasure, seeping from my center and zipping up my spine, reaching toward my fingers and toes and settling warm in my chest.

With a few more thrusts, Levi finishes. A moan, primal, leaves his mouth, and then we're a heap. He sinks into the bed, and I sink into him, and we're still connected, indistinct, nothing but heartbeats and heaving breaths.

Levi brushes hair away from my sticky forehead to press a kiss to my temple. "That was . . . to be honest, I don't have words for what that was."

"Yeah, that was . . ." I let the sentence linger unfinished. I understand exactly what he's not saying, because I'm not saying it either. That wasn't first-time, one-night-stand sex.

That was *I care about you* sex.

*I know you* sex.

His patience and attentiveness. How he responded to my discomfort. The teasing before. How safe I felt. It might have been, in another universe or on another timeline, *I love you* sex.

And so we don't try to find the words. Instead, Levi cleans himself up and throws the condom away. I gather my makeshift pajamas and put them back on. At some point, I fall asleep with the comforting weight of his arm around me and the belief that maybe I can learn to trust again. Buried under years of fear, it's a desire that's suddenly asking to be excavated.

Light pours in through cracks in the closed blinds, highlighting the curve of Levi's shoulders as they rise and fall with his breath. An arm draped across my stomach keeps me captive beneath the white fluff of the comforter. I claim the opportunity to study him while he sleeps: brown lashes resting on his cheeks, the strong line of his nose, a growing shadow of a beard, and the hint of his dimple—just a barely noticeable divot now, but one that holds promise for those who know how it transforms when he smiles. He's a beautiful man. Through and through, I'm learning.

"How long have you been staring at me?" He pops one eye open, his mouth still half-hidden by the pillow, the words muffled.

"How long have *you* been awake?"

He rolls to his side to face me, never moving his arm from my waist. "Long enough. Like what you see?" He gives a hopeful raise of a shoulder and a small tilt of his head. His grin deepens as he waits.

My eyes roll—one large, leisurely circle—and his smile grows. "Tell me about this." I bring a fingertip below his collarbone, to a scar about three inches long.

"That's from one of my very first projects. It was an indie film, low budget, but I figured any experience is good experience, right? I was too green to know they weren't following proper protocols."

I trace my finger across the smooth skin, back and forth from end to end. It flashes white for a second when I press on it.

"I was doubling for a fight scene." He's unbothered by my fingertip mapping the scar. "It started with hand-to-hand combat, throwing each other around, but ended with the guy opposite me pulling a knife."

I gasp, and he shakes his head.

"Oh, no—that was all part of the plan. We'd rehearsed how I'd dodge left to avoid his first strike. But when it came time to film, my momentum was off, and I didn't move quickly enough. He swiped me with the edge of the blade, and that's how I learned he wasn't using a prop knife or one that had been appropriately dulled. Eighteen stitches. Five years later, I think of the scar as a reminder—to work with teams who know what they're doing, people who honor protocols—and also to respect that this work is inherently dangerous."

He brings his hand from the dip of my waist to drape his palm over mine on his chest. Our fingers tangle inches above his heart, and it beats faster as we lie there for a moment with our eyes locked.

"Personally, I'm glad to be the one who sits out the hardcore stuff so people like you can jump in."

He taps his pointer finger three times against my skin before absentmindedly tracing small circles over my knuckles.

"Do you ever worry about it?" I ask. "About getting

seriously hurt, or not being able to do this long-term as your body ages, or messing something up that'll affect your quality of life forever?" It's an easy question to ask, but I know it's a big one to answer.

"Sometimes. It's hard not to worry, I think, especially when you hear stories about people getting injured, or worse, on set." His eyes scan the room as he collects his thoughts. "But at the end of the day, this is my one life. I'd rather spend it taking risks than playing it safe. You know better than anyone that a working body isn't guaranteed, no matter what a person does. I want to use my body in this way while I can, and what happens down the line is down the line. That's my thought process, I guess."

I reply with a slow nod, but my mind races to follow the thread: Levi prioritizes his job, risks and all. We both do. That's what this arrangement is about. Last night was . . . I'm still not really sure what last night was.

His breath feels cold on my skin when it hits the layer of nervous sweat that's sprung up on my neck.

"Are *you* worried about it?" he asks, with searching eyes and a tighter grip on the hand nestled with his.

"You've got enough people to worry about you." I dodge the question entirely because *am* I worried? Yes, but not about his stunt work or his safety—I've seen him perform. I'm worried about how comfortable our relationship has gotten and how real my feelings for him are becoming.

Sensing my hesitation, he slides his foot between my shins and wraps his ankle around my calf like a snake, pulling me closer. It brings our chests and hips flush. God, he feels good. Warm and strong and safe. But I feel myself tense anyway.

"Hey, no, no, no. No retreating into your head." He brings a hand to my face and presses his thumb into my chin, preventing me from turning my eyes from his. "That's outside world business, and we're not messing with the outside world right now, right? We're still in sleepover mode. So tell me, what happens the morning after a sleepover? Should I make eggs?"

The thought of Levi bringing me breakfast in bed, shirtless, with a dish towel draped over his shoulder? I pull my lip between my teeth with a nod.

His eyes dart down to my mouth. He leans forward and presses his lips to mine in a slow, intentional, lingering kiss. With a smile, he asks, "Or should I have you for breakfast?"

My brain says, *No, we should take a step back.*

My heart says, *No, don't let me get hurt.*

My mouth says, "Yes. Please," and he drags his mouth down my torso.

# XVII

## LEVI

Edwin and his Chrysler are failing to avoid the potholes on Hillsboro Road, and every time he hits one, it aggravates the lingering burn in my quads. Agreeing to a 7:30 a.m. hike the day after a fourteen-hour shoot was not a good move, as yesterday's call sheet had me riding a horse with a massive Greek spear in my hand. We ran the scene for thirty or more takes, covering all angles and ensuring the movement was accurate and compelling for each of the cameras. My body is spent.

"There's still time to turn around," Edwin says from the driver's seat when he hears me groan.

"And disappoint Ana? Not a chance."

"She's something, isn't she?"

"I'm pretty sure she's everything." The words come without conscious thought, and hearing them in my voice, from my mouth, startles me. *She's everything?* God, I need to rein myself in.

"She must be if you're up with the sun on your day off.

That's the best kind of sacrifice—making your woman happy."

"She's not . . ." I trail off. Am I going to argue that she's not my woman? After our sleepover last week, it feels like she is. I want her to feel like she is. "She's not hard to please," I say instead.

Because now that she's opened up to me the way she has, I can't stand the rumors that she's difficult. They're lies. She's not difficult; she's guarded. She's not inconsiderate; she's pulled in a million different directions. She's not prickly; she just has an instinct for self-preservation. The more she lets me in, the more I feel the bite of the way she's often treated. How she's been undermined by people who are supposed to be her peers. The closer she and I get, the more this knowledge gnaws at me.

"Hey, cowboy! You looked great on horseback yesterday." Ana walks toward me in the Radnor Lake parking lot.

"We might be in Nashville, but I'm sure not a cowboy." I pull her in for a quick hug. Wrapping my arms around her waist, my palms find the exposed skin at her lower back, below her cropped tank. "You sure this is how you want to spend the day?"

"Emily said this is *barely* a hike. It's just walking around the lake. It'll be good to get some fresh air before it gets too hot." She takes my hand and leads me in the direction of the visitor's center, though it appears to be closed. We study the posted map and decide to try the South Cove Trail, a meager 1.4 miles. Ana leads the way.

The sun streams through the canopy of trees surrounding the lake, speckling the ground with shadows and bursts of light. A bit of morning dew lingers in the smell of damp earth. It reminds me of early mornings back home. I take a long, deep breath.

"You truly were so impressive yesterday." She turns to meet my eyes. "Seeing you in your element, even just in the moments between my scenes, was really incredible."

"It was a nice break from all the hand-to-hand stuff we've been doing, even if my hips are worse for it today. I may need a piggyback ride at some point."

"At your service." She stops in front of me and bends slightly at the waist as if I might actually climb on her back. It puts her ass in line with my pelvis, and a flash of possibility, of taking her from behind, clouds my vision. I give her a gentle swat on the butt to encourage her to keep moving, and I feel gratified at the choked sound it prompts in her throat.

"So, is this a typical Saturday morning for you? Going on hikes?" I'm desperate to redirect my wandering thoughts.

Her head tilts back and forth, like she's weighing her answer. "Staying active is good for my joints and helps clear my head. To be honest, this sort of exercise—enjoying nature, not tracking the calories burned—is a reclamation of sorts. A middle finger to the years I spent trying to control my body. My teenage self would be proud."

She goes out of her way to step on a leaf, keeping her focus on the ground as she presses it underfoot. It doesn't crunch the way I know she wants it to.

"I imagine growing up in the industry made it difficult."

She swings her eyes back to mine. "Want to hear something really fucked up?"

"Always. Don't we all want to know the secret ugly stuff, if we're being honest?"

"'Ugly' might be too tame for this." She takes a deep breath and looks around to confirm we're alone. This is *that* kind of thing. I catch up to her so we're side by side.

"When I was thirteen, just a year into my acting career, I had an agent named Roy. God, even the name sounds skeevy coming out of my mouth. He and my mom controlled everything about my life at the time—the roles I auditioned for, what sort of clothes I wore, who I was allowed to be seen with. And I get it. I was a minor. I needed adults to navigate the business stuff for me. But Roy was very concerned about how my body was changing as I entered my teen years. He made constant comments about me *filling out* and *getting round in the hips* and shit like that."

"A grown man was saying that to you when you were *thirteen*?" I feel my eyes narrow, my brows pinch. Bile starts to rise in my throat.

"And somehow that's not the fucked-up part, if you

can believe it. Every morning, my mom would give me a protein shake. She said it would help me avoid growing pains because it had magnesium, maybe potassium, or something. I drank them for two years before I learned they were SlimFast shakes with a dose of laxatives. Roy and my mom decided they'd 'keep me thin' so I could continue to book roles—and make them money—playing younger than I was. Get the cute little sidekick jobs that had become my niche because, clearly, they weren't confident I was cut out for anything else. It was *for my career*, they said. *We were just trying to help*, and all that bullshit. The minute I turned sixteen, I filed for emancipation and got a new agent."

"You know that's abuse, right?"

"If you ever see a headline about me being estranged from my family, now you know why." Her shoulders lift in a shrug. "So yeah, like I said—my relationship with food, exercise, the way I view my body—it's tough for me, because even my mother didn't think I had what it took to be successful unless I looked a certain way."

"And yet here you are, filming the biggest role of your career."

"I hope she sees my face everywhere. And my *hips* everywhere."

She laughs, and the rage-filled heat that had been building behind my eyes softens and settles in my chest. Everything feels right when she laughs. I want more of it, and I want more of her. I want to know everything.

"And then what? What were those years like between leaving home and *Athena's War*?"

"Lots of peanut butter sandwiches," she says with a wink. "First, I found Emily—she was trying to get her foot in the door as a manager. I needed a place to stay and a new direction for my career, and she gave me both. I swear, we were fueled by spite and just enough delusion to hustle our way into rooms that weren't meant for us those first few years. She convinced me I could play anything. The girl next door in *She's All Mine*. A bombshell in that streaming frat house series—*Tight Quarters*. The romantic lead in *Match Made in Heaven*. She won't take no when it comes to my career—from me or anyone else."

"And suddenly I'm regretting never watching *Tight Quarters*."

She smiles, and now I'm the one feeling warm. "Making the transition from child star to respected adult actor is . . . It's not easy. With *Athena's War*, I felt like maybe—finally—I'd done it. They wanted me for the title role, this really meaty role, that wasn't about my looks or sex appeal. And then the story about Colt dropped."

I guide us left at a fork in the path. Ana dodges a fallen branch and shrugs, like I know what happens next in the story.

"Well, as fun as it's been trauma-dumping on you, can we talk logistics for the *People* interview on Friday morning? You have the details?"

"You mean, did my agent Sherry call me, absolutely

giddy, to tell me—at least three times—that we booked a two-page spread? She also gave me a ten-minute crash course in media training that we'll have to hope is enough."

"It'll be fine." Ana brings an arm around my waist. She fits perfectly in the space under my shoulder. "Have you done press like this before?"

"You know I haven't. You take the lead, and I'll be the strong, silent type."

"Well, the public thinks you're sweet, protective, loyal, and handsome. So do that."

"Do *you* think I'm handsome?"

"Right now, I think you're fishing for a compliment."

"And if I am?"

She rolls her eyes, but without conviction. "You're more than handsome, Levi. You're—"

"The most attractive man you've ever seen."

"And humble too!" She elbows my ribs. "You know, it's . . . this has been different from what I expected. This thing with you and me."

"Go on," I say, tucking her closer to me.

"I expected it to feel like a chore. Like another task to keep my career running smoothly. Another item on the checklist: costume fitting, personal training session, date with Levi, phone interview, and whatever else. I thought it would be another thing to budget energy for, but instead, I always leave you feeling . . . better. Buoyed."

She kicks at a rock in our path. I wrap my hand around her shoulder and squeeze.

"It's been surprising to me too. I assumed you'd be hard to work with."

"You mean the press didn't tee me up as sweet and loyal?" She laughs.

"They've got you all wrong. I'm not sure how you do it, putting up with this characterization of you that feels so obviously false. It must be tough."

"Honestly, it's not. It's something I value, keeping the soft parts of myself hidden from public consumption. There's so little that's mine after all these years. I'm not eager to give myself up to folks who can't be trusted."

When I realize the implication of her words—that she trusts *me*—anticipation, excitement, and fear clash in my gut, like that top-of-the-roller-coaster feeling of being high on the excitement of what comes next . . . but knowing that the danger is what makes it thrilling. That's where we are. The push and pull between the promise of how good this could be if it all goes well, and the awareness of how bad it could be if it doesn't.

Like if the tabloids somehow find out how this started between us.

Or if she hurts me.

Or if I hurt her.

Or if we let this become real and then it flames out, and I make a fool of myself before my career even really begins.

Like if I screw this up and lose the opportunity to work with Colt on his next film.

Fucking Colt. It crashes through me, the knowledge that *this* is the moment I should tell her what he said. I should get everything out in the open while we're alone and she's sharing about how rare it is for her to confide in people. After she opened up about her mom and Roy, I want her to know she can trust me—that I'm looking out for her.

But right now she's smiling. She's got the role of her dreams, and we're pressed together beneath the trees on our day off. Do I really want to ruin the moment for her? We're in a bubble I don't want to pop.

"I get the feeling *you're* the one stuck in your head this time," Ana says, interrupting my mental game of tug-of-war.

"Busted," I reply.

"Want to talk about it?"

*Now would be the time.*

"No."

"Want to kiss about it?"

I meet her eyes and, God, they're clear, like her feelings aren't the tangled mess mine are. We've been on this trail for twenty-five minutes, walking leisurely without seeing another soul. We could kiss about it if we want to. *How good this could be*, I think again.

She looks around before pulling us off the path and behind a maple. Then she turns to face me and inches up on her toes to bring her lips closer to mine. I slide an arm around her and tug her to me, our bodies flush, and drop my mouth to hers. I inhale coffee and coconut and the smell of nature on her skin. Her hands tug at the hair on the nape of my neck, and I smile into the kiss. She's figured out how much I love it when she does that. I groan and slip my hand under her tank, spreading my fingers across her back. She shivers when I do.

Her tongue glides along my lips and then into my mouth. What starts tender becomes urgent and demanding, both of us grasping at whatever skin we can find, licking and biting, and grinding with the contact. I grab her by the hips and walk her backward until she's up against a tree, notching my thigh between her legs. She sighs at the pressure.

"Sometimes . . ." she says, tilting her chin up to meet my gaze. Her eyes are soft but hungry—a mix of tenderness and need that has me hot from head to toe, bright and prickling like static under my skin. "Sometimes talking helps clear my head. But other times *doing* helps even more."

I answer her with another kiss, letting my hands roam her body. She wraps her arms around my neck. I grip her legs and lift them around my waist, the steadying press of my thigh still braced against her center. Almost immediately, Ana starts rolling her hips to rub herself against me. The moan she lets out, the moan she tries to muffle in my neck, takes root in my ear and shoots straight to my cock.

"Here's what we're going to do, then," I say. "I'm going to keep kissing you, and you're going to do whatever you need to make yourself feel good. I'm going to focus on you." I slide her body up and down my leg, prompting another moan. "And you're going to focus on you. And you're going to come just like this, where anyone could see you, because the idea of someone catching you—of seeing you out of control—turns you on as much as it scares you. Tell me I'm right."

"Less talking," she replies, but I don't miss her nod. I want her to keep collecting small pieces of evidence, like tiles for a mosaic, until she can see the picture clearly: She doesn't have to be anything but herself to be liked or valued. To be loved.

I capture her mouth with mine, and we settle into a deep kiss. She hums, and I feel it in the back of my throat as if it were my own. She rolls her hips into me, using her arms around my neck for leverage to grind against my leg. I encourage the movement with my hands on her hips, my fingertips pressing into the gloriously soft flesh where they meet her ass. Helping her move up and down just enough to have her whimpering into my mouth as her pleasure escalates. The feel of her, warm and wet against me, even through her leggings, is enough to make my next words come out choked.

"That's it, sweetheart," I whisper into her lips between drawn-out, wet kisses. "Use me. I can't wait to feel you come like this."

"Levi," she says on an exhale before collapsing into my chest. Her forehead falls to my sternum, and her arms hang lazily around my neck. Deep breaths in and out, and I keep my leg pressed against her as she tremors.

We stay like that, spent and silent, until we hear the distinct crunch of leaves under approaching footsteps.

"Shit." Ana scrambles down my body. I move to block her from view as she adjusts her leggings and sweeps back her hair.

"You look prettier than I've ever seen you," I say, leaning against the tree.

"Barely put together after risking arrest for public indecency?" Her cheeks are flushed, her lips are plump and slick from my mouth, and there's something looser, freer, about her than I'd have guessed was possible.

"Nope," I reply. "Satisfied."

"Did it help?" We resume walking the trail hand-in-hand, like she didn't just soak my thigh. Like I didn't love making her climax in public.

"Help what?"

"Get you out of your head."

"This head is now completely empty in favor of the other." I laugh. "But honestly? Yeah. It did."

Because the what-ifs from before haven't disappeared, but I have no doubt that she's right here with me. And maybe that means we can keep each other safe.

## ACCESS LA

### Levi Stephens's Sister Speaks Out! The Shocking Message From His Family

By Jessica Anders

Trouble at home? Rebekah Stephens, sister of Hollywood's newest man on the scene, Levi Stephens, bares the truth about his fame in a new TikTok video—the sibling's first, and currently only, appearance on the app.

In the seventy-second clip, Rebekah, the third of the family's four children, delivers an impassioned plea from a written script held in front of her.

"On behalf of the Stephens family, we understand there is growing interest in our son and brother, Levi Stephens. While we recognize that his work invites attention, the intrusive media requests, fan visits to Stephens Dairy, and unsolicited phone calls to our homes must stop."

She goes on to say that the family desires a smaller life than Levi has chosen for himself, and while he may consent to being a public figure, the family has no interest in joining him.

To that effect, Rebekah dropped a bombshell by disclosing that Levi left to film *Athena's War* without telling the family and that their lack of preparation for his new fame has made the situation even more difficult.

She closes the video by addressing the star directly, saying simply, "Levi, please call Dad."

As of Tuesday morning, the video has been viewed 2.8 million times, but the comment section has been disabled.

# XVIII

## ANA

The fluorescent overhead lighting has been left off in favor of lamps to make my trailer feel "warmer," and Levi and I are sitting, thighs touching and hands held, feeling more on display than we've ever been, while we wait for Monica Frank from *People* to get mic'd up for the video that will accompany the story.

I withdraw my hand from his to drape it over his thigh, my fingers skating across the inseam of his pants. It's a comforting, not sexual, gesture, but still he pulls in a sharp inhale.

"Hey." Lips next to his ear, I plant a kiss on his skin before whispering, "We've got this. Just be yourself. Everyone loves you. Once we're finished, we'll get out of here and do something fun." His eyes meet mine, and they're soft, a bit timid. Shards of light brown and green reflect the artificial light. I know he's more nervous than he would have been if his sister hadn't just, in a case of absolute shit timing, taken to the internet to throw him under the bus.

He covers my hand with his.

"This . . ." He gestures vaguely around the room as a producer tests for shadows on Monica's face. "This isn't normal for me."

Despite our initial plan to be coy with the press, my publicist, Marie, was all too pleased when this opportunity came across her desk, and his agent—accustomed to dealing with media for stunt doubles only when something goes wrong, I'd guess—was elated to conspire with her to make this happen. It would've been great for Levi to start with a smaller outlet to get his bearings and shake off some of the nerves. Alas.

"We're ready!" Monica drops onto a stool directly across from us. "So, we're hoping to keep this casual—chat back and forth, talk about the movie, your relationship, what's next, all that good stuff. The interview will be edited and condensed into a two-page print spread and digital feature."

"Understood." I toss a section of hair behind my shoulder.

"Let's start with *Athena's War.* Ana, this is your first lead role in an action film, and Levi, this is your first full-length film credit. How are you both feeling?"

"Excited. Grateful. Proud." I jump in. "This movie is special—and not just because of what it's meant for the both of us." I turn to meet his gaze for a brief moment.

"It's a story about being uniquely qualified for the task ahead of you and claiming it boldly. Most action films prioritize male dominance, and the female lead—if there is one—shows up in a skintight outfit and exists solely to support the male lead."

She nods with understanding as I continue. "In *Athena's War*, my character is a visionary—a woman who is both goddess of warfare and keeper of order. She represents wisdom and strategy—traits we often ascribe to men—but also historically feminine pursuits like weaving. She's a woman as complex as any of us, and I'm excited about the impact this will have on audiences who haven't seen that reflected in a movie like this before."

"An action movie is outside of your usual repertoire. Most of us know you for projects like Timmy Gray's pre-*Gatsby* comedies and rom-coms, like *Made from Scratch*," Monica says.

"It is new for me, but a role like this is something I've been working toward for years. Levi has too." His palm squeezes mine, and I squeeze back, an attempt to pass the figurative baton.

"Absolutely." He sits up a little taller. "I'm new to films of this scale, but I've been building up to this for the last six years. If you count doing tricks in my backyard as a kid, a lot longer."

He grins, but as Monica's eyes flash with interest, the color drains from Levi's face. He's one sentence in and has opened the door to a topic he wants to avoid.

She knows it too. “Your childhood, based on what I’ve read, seemed rather idyllic.”

“Well, there’s a lot to be said for growing up in a small town and learning the value of hard work and manual labor.”

“When did things begin to fracture with your family? When you took this job? Or were cracks showing before?”

“I’m not here to talk about that.”

My face wants to twist into a grimace at how he shut down the question—he sounded defensive—but I can’t let it. Instead, I squeeze his thigh and add a cheerful lilt to my voice. “What I see in Levi is a man who’s committed to achieving his goals. We’re similar in that way. I’m so grateful to our wonderful director, Francesca Stella, for seeing this trait in both of us when it came time for final casting.”

“And of course, Levi’s resemblance to Colt Haggerty must’ve been a key part of the decision,” Monica says as she angles her body toward me and drapes a hand over her knee, like we’re all sharing a secret. “This resemblance got you in trouble before filming had even started.”

I keep my smile soft and my voice upbeat, but my blood is boiling. “It’s an interesting phrase, *‘Got you in trouble.’* Something was reported that was untrue, but that’s nothing new. I’m not dwelling on it.”

My words are emphatic, definitive. My intention is to give her nothing, to shut down the line of questioning.

“My issue,” Levi says, and my heartbeat picks up. *Oh,*

*God, please no.* "Is that only Ana, quote, *got in trouble*. She was the one reduced to her looks in all the coverage. She's the one who gets blamed when a rumor like that surfaces."

My fingers dig into the flesh of his thigh, willing him to stop talking before his words get twisted around and spit out in print with a different meaning.

Ignoring my plea, he continues. "Listen, this sort of reporting—there's a double standard."

"You mean how the vitriol came down on Ana and not Colt, in this instance?"

*No. No, no, no. Don't answer that.*

"Exactly."

Cold air rushes through my nostrils as I inhale a centering breath.

Monica nods, and her eyes bore into mine, waiting for a response, but I wait her out.

"Your relationship went public after this. What's it been like since?"

Levi turns toward me and runs a thumb over the back of my hand. The comfort of it brings me back down into my body. "It's been a privilege to get to know a side of Ana the public doesn't see."

He's right—he knows me and sees me like so few people do. Like maybe no one else does. But that's a gift I've given him, and it's one I'm not giving to *People*. They don't deserve my vulnerability.

Monica turns her attention to me, waiting for my

response to her question. I inhale and refocus. "For all the moments we've been in front of cameras—both on set and off—we've also had plenty of time to ourselves. Filming on location has given us opportunities to connect away from the fishbowl that is Los Angeles. There's something special about that."

"Would you say it's getting serious between you?"

"No, there's no rush to put a label on this," I reply. I feel the heat of Levi's gaze on my face but don't turn toward him. "We're just having fun and enjoying each other's company."

The pulse in his wrist picks up at the phrase *having fun*. His hand flexes under mine.

Telling this reporter is one thing, but *is* that what we're doing here? Yes and no. I know there's more to it than that, and judging by the way his body responded, he does too.

"And after *Athena's War*, what's next for you both?"

Levi jumps in. "My hope is to have a long career in stunt work, but for now, all my focus is on *Athena's War*. Thinking beyond that would be a distraction."

Even though I know what he's saying is true, and even though I downplayed our relationship—or whatever this is—less than a minute before, his words still twist in my gut.

"What about you, Ana? What's next?"

I hope my face, with a soft smile that feels plastered on, doesn't betray me as I answer. "I'll echo Levi—my focus is on doing my best work on this film, giving it the attention it deserves at release, and enjoying myself in the process, both professionally"—I turn to face him—"and personally."

Monica returns my smile as she turns off her mic. As I count down to when I can call Emily to start damage control for this disaster of an interview.

# XIX

## LEVI

The fan hands the phone to me, and I aim the camera, framing her and Ana in the middle of one of the arched windows along the front wall of the Finch. Ana's still in her *People* interview look—a short-sleeve purple sweater, wide-leg jeans, and makeup that even I can tell took a long time—and the woman who approached our table is wearing a bedazzled cowboy hat and a "Last Fling Before the Ring" T-shirt. She's one of the many bachelorettes who appear in this city every Friday, and her crew of hype girls, all in matching pink, sits at a large circular booth next to the bar.

"How's this?" I hand the phone back. The bride-to-be tilts her head to the side and appraises the photo.

She shrugs like she's disappointed with the shot but recovers quickly. "I can't wait to see the movie. Hard to believe I'm going to be a married woman then!" She turns and makes her way back to her squealing group. I chuckle at the sight of it, the flamingo-colored mass of energy.

"Can you even imagine having that many friends?" Ana is incredulous.

"If I'd stayed in Ohio and proposed to my college sweetheart like my parents wanted, I might have become one of the guys in the . . . what was that bus called with the hot tub in the back we saw on the way here? The Music City Party Tub? I can hear the Kane Brown cranking now."

She pulls the side of her lip between her teeth like she's trying to picture it before a boisterous laugh escapes her. It causes the table next to us to turn their eyes in our direction.

"Sorry!" Ana whispers and scrunches her nose. "Didn't know this would be a tough crowd."

"Maybe we should've asked Edwin to bring us to lunch somewhere less . . . on display."

"Yeah, that interview definitely took it all out of me."

"How do you think it went?" I'm twirling a straw in my glass of water and hoping I'm projecting a casualness I don't particularly feel.

"For your first real media experience?" She shifts a little in her seat. "It . . . wasn't all bad."

"But some of it was bad?"

"The stuff about Colt and the double standard—they can take those quotes out of context. I'd be surprised if they didn't, honestly."

"But it was the truth—you weren't treated fairly, and people should know that. I'm not worried about it." An itchy feeling prickles the back of my neck, and I press my fingers into the muscle there.

"It was very white-knight of you. And risky. Who knows, maybe it'll be fine. I guess I'm just not used to having people look out for me."

"Is that part of *having fun*? Looking out for each other?" I don't intend it to come out sounding as snarky as it does. Something flares in her eyes, and she folds her hands on the table.

"Are you really going to take that personally? What was I supposed to say, Levi? That we're working together and occasionally sleeping together and sometimes sharing pieces of ourselves that no one else gets to see? The story is that we're dating—we're an on-set romance just significant enough for us to be needled into doing an interview together. Everyone who reads the story will understand our relationship is tied to the film. No one expects it to *last*."

She bites her bottom lip, like she didn't mean to bring as much snark either. She takes a deep breath. Sighs. "To be honest, I'm not sure what we are to each other. And you certainly didn't have a problem using this interview to your benefit, leaning into your career ambitions, so you have no room to talk."

She's right, but I only went so hard because she started down the path, and I felt compelled to follow. Right? "Can't both things be true?" I drop my voice down a notch. "We're spending time together to benefit our careers *and* something is happening between us that doesn't feel fake anymore. Or am I alone in feeling that?"

Ana brings a hand to her drink. The glass is dotted with beads of sweat. Maybe it's feeling the tension in the air too. She swipes some of the condensation away with a pass of her thumb. "I . . . no."

"No, I'm not alone? Or no, you're not feeling this too?"

"I don't want to get hurt," she answers softly.

"I don't want to hurt you."

"Then don't." She reaches for my hand and slots her fingers between mine. "I don't know what to call this—or maybe I'm scared to name it—but I feel it, and it's new, and my nature is to downplay it so it can't grow too big, too out of my control. I meant it when I said I'm not thinking about what's next. Right now, I'm here and learning that maybe it's possible to have a career that doesn't come at the expense of my personal life, or a personal life that doesn't come at the expense of my career. It's scary for me. Scary to let myself hope."

Her eyes dart back and forth, scanning mine, and she's asking something of me. It's the same look from the day at my apartment with the pizza dough. *Be patient with me while I find my new shape.*

I hope she sees that I'm trying.

"It's scary as hell for me too, Ana. I know it's dumb. I was just worried you weren't on the same page. If you want to step back . . . we can do that. The last thing I'm trying to do is come into your life and make it complicated."

Because isn't that what I always seem to do? Make choices that hurt the people I love in some way?

"You're not making my life complicated, I promise. Let's keep doing what we're doing—whatever it is—and we'll see how it evolves. No pressure. I like spending time with you. I want to keep spending time with you."

Relief washes over me. "Here's to *having fun* together." I lift my drink for a toast, and she levels her pretty green eyes at me before bringing her glass to mine. A smile curls the edges of her lips, and it unfurls something in my chest.

**reddit.com/r/BattleOfTheGodsFilms**

**u/okayamethyst**

**Ana Barlow is ruining the movie before it even comes out**

Before you jump on me, I tried to give her the benefit of the doubt. Ngl she's been funny in her best friend / dumb blonde roles, and I even thought she was pretty good as a lead in *Match Made in Heaven* (don't come at me, I watched it on a plane). I was surprised and kinda disappointed when they cast her for Athena but I figured Francesca or someone at the studio must've known what they're doing. Now I'm not sure I'm even going to see the movie because I know she's gonna piss me off the whole time.

Her showing herself off with selfies at the gym and hiking and whatever is completely self-absorbed. It's like every chance she can get, she's putting herself on display. Meanwhile, Colt is lying low, like someone who actually gives a shit about the movie. She needs to give more attention to the film and less to her image. And this sudden, super convenient relationship with the stunt double? The timing is sus. Idk, it's just rubbing me the wrong way.

**u/cheaptrickery_18** For me the last straw was the *People* interview where she whined about the tabloids. Girl, shut up—they're the ones giving you publicity!! It's like she thinks she's too good for it which is wild because until now she's literally only had like two starring roles, whereas Colt's an effing legend. She's a notoriously hard to work with rom-com B-lister, and he's action star royalty. They're such a weird pairing for this movie. And agree about it being suspect with the double. Make it make sense!!

**u/okayamethyst OP** You're so right about Colt

**u/cheaptrickery_18** Thx for the upvote

**u/georgiamindseye** Dont know if anyone is still following this thread, but jic: did you guys see the Deuxmoi post? That the Ana stunt bro relationship is for real fake? Someone at Swole in LA said they were putting on quite a show before filming and that no one was buying it. Ridic.

# XX

## ANA

Emily is trailing me, spouting encouraging platitudes as I pace the living room of this rental house, back and forth between a linen-covered sofa and built-ins that hold a massive TV I've never turned on. "It's fine. You're fine. We can figure this out."

"Nothing about this is fine." Agitation claws up my throat and puts my voice in a vise grip. Every word comes out like it's being squeezed through a fist. "Is Levi coming? Please tell me he's coming."

"Any minute now. He left as soon as I texted."

At that moment, the doorbell chimes with a cheerful little ditty. It echoes through the house, bouncing off the walls and windows like a personal affront. Emily runs to answer it.

"Hey, Em," comes the voice from the front hall. It's deep and comforting and a bit winded.

A shuffle of shoes being removed and placed by the door buys me one more moment to compose myself.

Levi rounds the corner and finds me stalking back and forth, marking a path in the silk rug. "Hey, sweetheart," he says, his brows pulled tight.

Emily does jazz hands behind him to get my attention, mouthing, *"Sweetheart?!"* with wide eyes. I shake my head. Now's not the time.

Levi steps in front of me, blocking my path, and places two heavy palms on my upper arms. The warmth of him seeps through my shirt and blooms on my skin. It acts like a tether, restraining my panic. I take a deep breath.

"Can we sit?" he asks, even though he's spinning me around and guiding my shoulders from behind before I have the chance to answer. We drop onto the couch, and I wonder, briefly, how anyone decides linen is the best material with which to upholster a sofa.

"How are you doing?" he asks, as though it's not abundantly clear by my pacing and breathing and overall demeanor.

"Been better."

Levi nods and wraps an arm around my waist to pull me into his side. Resting my head on his chest feels easy, natural. My cheek rises and falls with each of his breaths. "Emily said . . ." He rubs his fingers along my hip. "Want to tell me about it?"

"Fucking Deuxmoi got a tip about us. Everyone thinks—everyone *knows*—we're pretending." I tilt my face to meet his eyes, which are soft. Mine are bloodshot.

"I'm sorry, Doo-what now?"

"Oh my God, Levi, it's a celebrity gossip page. You're *such* a farm boy."

He ignores my dig. "But we're *not* pretending, right?"

I clock the way Emily clears her throat and excuses herself from the room, mumbling under her breath about retrieving a dress from the seamstress. She holds my eye contact for a beat before turning into the hallway. *You'll be fine*, her look says. *You always are.*

I have no such confidence.

"Was I wrong to think we agreed last week at the Finch that something real is growing here? Maybe we should keep showing up like we enjoy spending time together—because we do—and wait for people to move on to their next conspiracy theory."

"They might move on, but people don't *forget*. They think I'm a liar, and in a few days' time they'll corroborate the story somehow, and there will be another round of 'Manipulative Ana Barlow' headlines."

"Hey, slow down." Levi glides his hand down the length of my arm. This time, it does nothing to calm my racing heart or stifle the words flying out of my mouth.

"And then there's the same old shit about me being vain and controlling. Of course, Colt gets to do whatever he wants, and everyone fawns over him. I work out, and I'm a show-off; Colt's an arrogant asshole who's high on his own supply, and he's a hero. Rinse and repeat every fucking news cycle. For once, I'd like him to be on the other side. Maybe that makes me a bitch, but I can't will myself to care."

"You're not—" Levi pauses, fills his lungs, and holds for a beat before releasing. His fingers drum staccato on my arm.

"What?" I ask.

He clenches his hands into fists but doesn't respond.

"What is it? Please, just say it."

The nervous energy in his hands spills out of his lips: "Colt's a piece of shit, honestly."

"Believe me, I know that."

Levi pulls a face, like the words cause him physical pain. "No, he's been a piece of shit to *you*."

He runs his hand through his hair, that anxious tick betraying him just before his mouth does. "He told me he tried to get you off the film." The lines on his face deepen. "When the story broke in the *Star*, he asked Francesca directly to fire you."

My heart stops. The world freezes, and his words hang in the air, suspended and swirling while everything else stays motionless. After a moment, I blink myself back into my body and turn to face him.

The swirling begins again. Heat floods my chest, my face, my knuckles. At first, it's embarrassment, but it shifts quickly into anger.

Anger at Colt.

Anger at being a pawn.

Anger at the backstabbing.

*Anger at Levi.*

"Wait. Back up. You knew he'd tried to get me fired and didn't tell me?" I stand up from the couch and resume my trail on the carpet. "This is a joke, right? You're joking."

"I thought maybe you already knew, and if you didn't, I wouldn't be doing you any favors by telling you. But whether or not you knew, what would you have done differently? Ana, you kept the role. You kept the press at bay, just like you wanted. Isn't that what's important?"

He leans forward with his forearms on his thighs, his hands clasped. He ought to drop his head between his knees in shame while he's at it.

"So you decided I didn't deserve to know that my co-star tried to ruin my career?" I seethe. "That ignorance is bliss, or some shit? I can't believe this."

"What was the alternative?" His voice is steely behind clenched teeth. "I tell you something I heard—a plan that *didn't actually happen*—for what? I was trying to protect your feelings, and listen, I only decided to tell you now because you need to know that he's been a bitch, not you. At the end of the day, his plan didn't work. Your plan did. That's what matters."

*That's what matters.* Are the words Levi's or Roy's? Levi's rant brings me back in time, to my mom's kitchen table fourteen years earlier, until I feel the hard back of a wooden chair bruising my spine and I see my former agent's face, his lips forming the words, across from me.

Both him and my mother trying to convince me that what they did—what they kept from me—*wasn't a big deal* and how *the ends justify the means* and I *came out ahead*, didn't I?

Sticky sweat rises on my neck, the same as it did that day, and I feel the same roiling, churning in my stomach.

I stop marching and stand in front of Levi, the person who I thought was showing me, day after day, that I could trust him.

What a sucker I am.

"You had the choice," I say, resentment clinging to each word, "between being honest with me and protecting your prospects. I'm not dumb, Levi. I know what we're doing here. I suggested that this arrangement could be mutually beneficial for our careers, so let me be clear: I'm not upset that you were trying to get ahead by playing your cards right. It's that you were willing to do it *at my expense*. I asked you to play this game with me so I could maintain control over just one piece of my life. Withholding something like this from me? That's *you* taking control, and that wasn't the deal."

I run my tongue over my teeth and swallow against a dry throat. He's looking at me, and I want him to fight. Fight with me. Fight *for* me.

"You're right," is all he says.

"That's it? *You're right?*" I scoff. "God, you don't get it. I told you about my mom, Levi. About Roy. About how crushing it was to learn that they were making decisions behind my back and then turning around and claiming

I was better off not knowing. In reality, they kept things from me because it benefited them. Sound familiar?"

"I'm not your mom and Roy." He drags his eyes up to meet my gaze before darting them back to study his hands. "I'm not, and you know it. It was a passing remark that Colt made, without any context, and you kept the role, so why bring it up? I didn't want to make you upset, and I didn't want to risk messing things up. With Colt *or* with you. That's all."

"And yet here we are, and I'm upset, and you've messed things up with me anyway."

He nods, and his lack of response whips the churning in my belly into a cyclone—a wind shear of anger, sudden and forceful. If I took a minute to breathe, or think, or ground my feet on the earth, I'd wonder if I'm overreacting. But I can't. Instead, the words punch out of my mouth. "All I've ever wanted—needed—is for someone to choose me. Not beautiful Ana Barlow, not famous and thin and wrapped in designer clothes Ana Barlow, but the version you'd been uncovering. You had her. I gave that version of myself to you, and I was stupid enough to believe I could trust you to hold it. I thought we were a team, and I was wrong. Because you don't care about me—people who care tell each other things like this. Instead, you wanted a stepping stone and were content to put your foot on my neck to give yourself a leg up. Just like everyone else."

He sits there, wringing his hands. Dark eyebrows pinched in toward his nose. Lips pulled together. No hint of the dimple I love—*loved*—on his cheek. He clears his throat and swallows. My gaze traces it down the column of his neck.

"Where do we go from here?" he asks, as though we're business partners building a road map for our quarterly goals. As though he didn't just break my heart.

"There's no need to pretend anymore. They outed us." I release a petulant huff. "Turns out I can't even *fake* my way to being beloved by the public. Should've left you out of it and saved myself all this mess."

"Ana, we don't have to . . ."

"Don't have to what, Levi?" I bring my hands to my neck, to the chronic pain that lives there.

"Forget it, I'm sorry." He gets up from the couch and heads for the door. I follow him there, and he turns to me. "I didn't mean to hurt you."

"You and the rest of them."

He winces at the words. "Can we keep things normal at work?"

"Yes, Levi, I can be professional at my place of employment. I've spent two decades pretending to feel what I don't feel and pretending not to feel what I do. This won't be any different."

He nods.

"Oh, and I'm not going to jeopardize your standing with Colt, if that's what you're asking."

"It wasn't." He slips on his shoes, bending to tie the

laces and splaying the muscles in his shoulders and back. Damn stuntman build.

"See you on set." I open the door and gesture for his exit.

"See you," he says, and he steps across the threshold.

# XXI

## LEVI

"I'm a selfish asshole." My head leans against the cool glass of the car's window. Edwin meets my eyes in the rearview mirror and gives a soft, if pitying, smile.

"Do you want to know why?" I ask him. If I'm going to turn this car into a rolling confessional, he might as well get the full story. There's no one else to talk to about this anyway. I've alienated my friends and family back home. Everyone in this town is a stranger to me, except for my fellow castmates, and involving even more of the *Athena's War* crew in this mess is not an option. But Edwin's here, and luckily for me, he nods his head. Either that, or he's not brave enough to say no when I'm so clearly in need of a sounding board.

"I'm an asshole because I put myself, and my fear, over being honest with the woman I care about. I kept something from her." A sigh escapes as I tap my head against the glass in self-punishment.

Edwin pulls into a turning lane, his signal clicking. "Do you want my opinion?"

"I'll take anything you can give me."

"I've been married for twenty-eight years. My wife and I, we got married young. Too young, looking back, but that means we've lived a whole lot of life together. I've made my fair share of mistakes, slept some nights on the couch, raised my voice when I shouldn't have. I'm no expert, and Daisy—that's my wife—would probably tell you I'm not the best person to be giving relationship advice. But here's what I know: Loving someone is complicated."

A huff and a nod are all I can give. Complicated is an understatement, and I don't have the energy to tell him I'm not sure "love" is where Ana and I have been.

He meets my eyes in the rearview mirror. "When a woman is upset, there are two pieces of the puzzle to consider: The thinking and the doing. Took me about a decade and a half to learn this, so count yourself lucky you're hearing it now." He chuckles. "If Ana is anything like my wife, the doing matters far less than the thinking. For example, it's not the act of taking out the trash that matters to her. What matters is the consideration: That I noticed the trash can was full, that I recognized if I didn't take it out, I'm adding the task to her list. It feels like a simple chore, right? What's the big deal? It takes less than a minute to bring the bag to the curb. But it's not the task that really matters; it's that I thought about her. And when I think about her, what I do changes. You following?"

"Following."

"My hunch is Ana's upset because you didn't consider her."

The gray matter of my brain is melting. Hot, soupy mush as I try to untangle what he's saying. His wisdom isn't just about Ana, I fear.

"You're young. Inexperienced. You shouldn't beat yourself up about that. Like I said, it took me fifteen years to figure this out. Here's where it gets even more complicated, though. My guess is you probably *did* think about her, and at some point, you decided you didn't want to make her riled up about something that might not be a big deal. Do I have that right?"

"How could you possibly know that?"

"Because I do it too. Sometimes I make choices for my wife that I think are for her benefit, and then I feel good about myself. I'm protecting her, and all that. But you know what she sees?"

"Hmmm?"

"To her, it's infantilizing. She doesn't need me to make calls for her. She's a strong, smart woman, and she can make decisions for herself."

"Shit."

"Yep."

"I fucked this up."

"You aren't the first and won't be the last, I'm afraid." He winks at me through the mirror.

"Thanks, man. This is . . . thanks."

For the last ten minutes of our drive, thoughts whip in my brain. I think about Ana, about betraying her trust, about how to apologize. I think about my family, about my deep-seated belief that all I do is disappoint people. When I took this job, I thought choosing my career over my family and the farm was the issue. But maybe it was that I didn't consider—much less recognize—how that choice would affect them. Leaving without any sort of goodbye or acknowledgment, I considered them even less.

Or Ana's history of being lied to and then placated. I didn't truly consider that either when I chose to keep Colt's words to myself. And if what Edwin is saying is true—that people who mean something want to be considered, even if it doesn't change the outcome—the opposite is also true. Without that consideration, people think they don't mean anything.

This realization claws at my chest and squeezes my lungs.

# XXII

## ANA

"Cut! Take ten to reset."

My arms collapse at my sides the second the scene ends. Sweat sprinkles my forehead, my palms, and gathers beneath the draped linen covering my chest. My shoulders rise and fall as I catch my breath and take a moment to come back into myself. I slip out of Athena like she's a cloak I can drape carefully over my forearm until I need to put her back on.

"Ana, can you come here?" Francesca asks.

My eyes shift to her standing next to the primary camera, squinting as she watches playback. With tired steps, I make my way over.

"Take a look—when you're approaching Ares from behind, I'm not getting the full weight of your emotion because your face stays blocked by his shoulder a hint too long."

I see what she's saying and tell her as much.

"For the next take, try to swing wider so we can feel the anguish and the audience can dwell there, just for a second, before Ares notices you and the scene continues."

"Of course, that's a great call. Thank you, Francesca."

"Thank *you* for really digging in here; I know this isn't an easy scene to film."

"I want to get it right." I smile.

"I know you do."

I've been stewing on what to do with this Colt revelation, and I decide on my move. "Hey, could I stop by your trailer after the shoot today? I'd like to talk through something with you."

"As long as you don't mind a late night. In the meantime, go get something to drink, sit down for a minute. We'll be ready to go again in five." She shoos me toward craft services, and it's remarkable, really, how different it is having a female director on this film. It feels like all my weariness from years spent on sets with every note given through the male gaze has been erased in the months that I've been working under Francesca.

She's so different than I thought she'd be after that tense meeting in the conference room before filming started. She's focused, with high expectations for our performance, but she's also encouraging. More and more, I'm realizing that she's a lot like me, with a reflex to protect herself and what she's worked for. I think she recognizes it in me now too.

Cast and crew members hover around trays of muffins, veggies, and tubs of hummus. My eyes bounce around, looking for someone to hitch myself to, to engage in conversation with. But of course, they fall to him—he's right there, fifteen feet away, talking with Colt. My stomach drops to my toes.

God, he looks like everything I don't feel. Content, easy. He lets out an open-mouthed laugh, dropping his head back and bringing a hand to his chest, and it may as well be a bullet the way it tears through my gut. Being on set together is apparently no problem for him. And if it's no problem for him, I will make sure he knows it's no problem for me either.

My "Hey, guys!" as I approach the table comes out bright, a bit too sharp. I soften the tone. "Colt, how many more takes do you think we'll have today? I'd put money on six." I give him my best grin, one with megawatt teeth and smile lines crinkling around my eyes. "Six if we're lucky," Colt says. "I'll put a hundred down that it's ten plus. Want to shake on it?"

Our hands clasp. Levi's jaw flexes in my peripheral vision. I place my other palm on top, feigning warmth or nipping at Levi's ego, I'm not sure which. If it gets a rise out of him, he doesn't show it.

At *"Places!"* we perk up like dogs who've heard a whistle.

Colt puts a hand on my shoulder as he makes his way past me. Levi's presence is both silent and insistent, like a pregnant pause before a secret. Except, when it comes to Levi, he doesn't share secrets. Not with me, anyway.

"Ana, I—"

I turn back toward set without acknowledging his bid for my attention. It's time to get back to work, and he knows better than anyone that's what we're here for.

I drag my fingers across the storyboard hanging in Francesca's trailer. It maps the narrative arc of *Athena's War*, complete with sketches, production notes, and fabric samples used to inform costume design. It's like seeing the inside of someone's brain, looking at this. Everything we're doing on set—this story we're telling—started with her brilliant mind. It's incredible to witness.

She smiles, letting her eyes drift back and forth as I touch the two-dimensional plan we're bringing to life each day. "Crazy, isn't it, how an idea can turn into an outline, and then a script, and then a movie? It's easy for it to become so familiar you forget the magic of it—of creating something out of nothing."

"Yes . . . though filming this movie has felt *particularly* wild, and not always in a good way." I turn to face her, and she appraises me, her eyes skating over my expression.

She nods and lets out a breathy laugh. "This process

hasn't been what I expected either, though that's largely on the personal front."

I raise my brows, questioning.

She claims a small loveseat, and when she motions for me to sit, I take the one opposite. For a brief moment, I feel unsteady with déjà vu, the image of Levi and me sitting for our interview with *People*. How quickly things have changed.

Before I can lose the nerve, I say, "This may be unprofessional, but . . . Did Colt ask you to recast my role? Did he try to get me fired?"

She clears her throat and averts her eyes. "He did. And when the story broke with the *Star*, we were concerned about ongoing negative press . . . but he was stressed about his image, not about me, and certainly not the film. You could say it was a tipping point for us, that I didn't let you go. He's so used to getting whatever he wants without question. He didn't handle my decision very well."

"Levi and I got into a fight about it," I blurt, inserting my own heartache into the middle of hers with all the grace of a newborn giraffe.

"About the *Star*?"

"About whether he should have told me that Colt was gunning for me. He knew for weeks and kept it to himself."

Francesca shifts forward in her seat and brings folded hands between her knees. Compassion oozes from her stance, her eyes.

"You know, I wasn't sure what to make of it when you

two started up. It was a clever idea, by the way, to attempt this switcheroo with the press. It obviously impressed me enough to keep you on the film—and I've been thankful every day that I did. *And* your plan worked. But you know why it worked, right?"

Heat prickles at the back of my neck, and my nerves stand at attention. I don't answer, and she continues.

"It worked because I don't think it was ever actually fake between you and Levi. It was obvious from the start, to me and everyone else, that there was a connection between the two of you—friendly at first, and then something else. The charade with Levi worked because it wasn't a charade. Not really."

"I suppose it wasn't." I sink into the dense weight of that truth, like quicksand I'd like to disappear into.

"To be honest, seeing you two together, it was such a stark contrast to my marriage. My relationship with Colt has been deteriorating for a long time. I think part of me hoped that working on this film might fix things between us. Instead, the 24/7 proximity made it very clear, very quickly, that our marriage isn't fixable." She presses her hands into her thighs. "Keep this between us, of course. It's been a long time coming."

I nod, knowing her pain is of a different order of magnitude than my own. How could it not be? Theirs is a Hollywood unicorn, a decades-long relationship. Even so, she seems steady. Resolute.

"But the only way I know that our marriage isn't fixable,

and the reason why I can sit here and talk about it like this, is *because* we tried to fix it. For years, honestly. But you and Levi? My hunch is that it may be fixable. And don't you want to try? If only so you can know for sure?"

"But what if he doesn't want to try? And what if I . . . majorly overreacted and said some really awful things?"

"Who among us hasn't?" she says with a laugh. "Part of fighting for a relationship is taking responsibility when we do."

"Are you sure you're not a therapist moonlighting as a director?" I wipe at my damp eyes.

"Just someone who's been there. But I'll answer one more question, even though you didn't ask it. Why *did* I fight to keep you in this role?" She smooths a palm over her slicked-back bun. "Because you're tough—but in different ways than people seem to think you are. I saw that when you walked into that meeting with Colt and me. But you're also softer than people think. You're the full Athena package."

My jaw opens and closes, but all I can do is press the heels of my palms against my eyes. The tears pass the floodgates. It's not just Levi who sees and knows and appreciates me. Francesca does. And Emily does. And I think—finally—I can too.

"Now." She pats her hands against her thighs and stands up from the couch. "It's late, and we've got another early day tomorrow. Go get some sleep. Take a few days to figure out your feelings, and then talk through them with Levi. One thing I know for sure: 10 p.m. is never the right time to try to fix a relationship."

A warm wall of air hits me as I leave her trailer.

She's right. Maybe about everything.

# XXIII

## LEVI

Gray.

The countertops, the carpet, the accent chair. My mood.

Everything in this damn apartment lacks color. Even the knife block is charcoal, and glancing at it now—the memory of Ana in my kitchen as I reached behind her for it—makes me want to stab something. It's a small mercy that shooting days are long because every aspect of this place makes me think of her. On my couch, in my clothes, under my covers. Under my body. Being on set together is torture enough, only to come home and feel the ghost of her here. Thank God we only have a few more weeks in Nashville.

I climb into bed, eager to escape to wherever my mind might bring me tonight. Dreams seem to be the one place Ana's not. Looking for sweet relief, I burrow in, feeling a little like the pigs I grew up with, trying to get comfortable in the mud. I'm just as gross. But the sheets settle uncomfortably on my feet. My toes graze the cotton the wrong way. It's too hot, so I strip off my shirt, and then it's too quiet. The white noise app on my phone hums to life, and I try to get comfortable after plugging it back in to charge. The effort is futile. I lie there, eyes locked on the spackled ceiling.

Five days have passed since I ruined things with Ana, and seeing her today, watching her effectively ignore me on set—damn did it feel like shit. Or maybe *I* felt like shit. I can hear my dad's voice in my head: *Well, if it isn't the consequences of your own actions*. Don't I know it.

Worst of all for me—maybe best of all, for her—she seemed . . . fine. It's not that I want her to suffer. But feeling like this hasn't gutted her, when I'm practically disemboweled, makes it that much more harrowing. I need the chance to tell her I'm sorry, that I recognize how I made her feel by not considering her, and to see if there's any way we can try this again. To do that, though, I'd need her to be willing to talk to me.

Colt and I are both being filmed on horseback today, with his scenes shot up close at a slower speed, and mine shot wide at full gallop. Ana and her double are here, shooting the same way, and since we're on location outside of the city, there's no escaping her.

"Ready to get back in the saddle?" Colt asks as I stretch a forearm behind my head and press on my elbow with my opposite hand.

"If we were riding in saddles, sure. Any chance you can petition Francesca to rework the setting of the film to use modern tack?" I give him a raised eyebrow. We're running another battle scene, which means we have hours ahead bareback. He answers the question with a slap on my shoulder.

Wearing a wool cloak—what our costume designer calls a chlamys—the sun feels especially punishing. It's pushing ninety-five degrees, and there's only so much shade to be found under the production tent. I go looking for a bottle of water before my scene starts.

"Levi," a voice calls from behind me. My heart flips at the familiar tone, my body not yet conditioned to respond differently than it used to at the sound of Ana's voice. She catches up to me and places a hand on my arm. Heat sparks under her palm and shoots to my chest. I turn to face her, and the way the sun hits her cheekbones—shit.

"Hey, I know you're about to film, but I wanted to apologize for the other day."

*Which day?* I wonder, but I don't ask because she's talking to me, and isn't that the only thing I've wanted?

"When I made the bet with Colt. You tried to get my attention, and I ignored you. That wasn't professional of me, and I know we discussed keeping things professional on set. I'm sorry about that. And I won the bet, if you were wondering."

I nod, letting her words seep in.

"I guess I wasn't in a place to have a conversation with you then," she continues, "but if you want to talk, we can."

"I'd like that," I reply, conjuring up a smile that I pray feels approachable, apologetic, but not overeager. "If you're up for it, there's a great Greek place I heard about." She eyes me with a raised brow. "Yes, I see the irony," I add.

"Oh, well, I don't know if . . ." Her eyes shoot down, tracing the straps of the sandals on my feet.

Too much, too soon. Before I can backtrack, clarify that I didn't mean a date, just a place to talk, our lead animal trainer's voice interrupts.

"Stephens! You ready?" He's waiting with Nesbitt, Ares's horse for the film. I give him a thumbs-up before turning to Ana. "Duty calls. We'll find a time to talk?"

"OK," she agrees, while I search her face for a smile she doesn't give me.

"Alala!" The war cry burns on its way out of my throat, using up every ounce of oxygen in my lungs. Nesbitt thunders underneath me, his legs exploding with power in every stride. My quads hug his body, clenched, as we gallop forward. Spear in hand, head thrown back, I'm leading an army of Greek soldiers in their attempt to recapture Athens.

"Alala!" we repeat, and wild fury twists inside me. My adrenaline compensates for the ache in my hips, the spasm trying to grip my bicep as I pull back to throw the javelin. It lands exactly where it should, and I dig my heel into Nesbitt's side to urge him forward. The thunderous sound of hooves grows louder, all in unison save for one horse, slightly off rhythm. Still, we race toward the opposing mass of warriors: Athena's army. The taste of dripping sweat stings my tongue as we charge ahead, tracking according to plan, and then—

The horse behind us clips Nesbitt's ankle.

He shudders and rears up, lifting his front legs from the ground.

I grasp on to his mane and try to tighten the grip of my legs around the barrel of his ribs, but in slow motion, I fly off the horse, legs cartwheeling overhead.

Dust obscures my sense of where I am in space.

*Crash, crunch.*

Black.

# XXIV

## ANA

"CUT!"

Production halts immediately, and I know this is *bad*. Every muscle in my body tenses, and my heart pounds against my ribs. Cast members guide their horses back to the holding pen, and a trainer runs over to handle Nesbitt. Flashes of red-wool costumes and chestnut-brown tails clutter the scene, and I can't see Levi amid the chaos, even as my eyes strain and dart to where he should be. Medical rushes in, and for a moment—after the crew retreats and before our med team intervenes—I spot him. He's alone. A tangled heap on the ground.

"Levi!" The shout escapes my throat as my legs pick up speed to make their way to him.

"No, let them work." Colt wraps his arm around my middle. My body strains against his grip.

"I just"—I struggle against him—"need to see that he's OK!" The effort is futile. "LET GO OF ME."

He doesn't know about my joints, about how easily

I bruise, about how careful I need to be with my body. About the risk I incur with him grabbing me like this. "Get off of me! I don't need you to restrain me. I can control myself."

"You're clearly *not* in control, and it's not your job to make sure Levi's OK. That's medical's job, and they're the best in the business. Take a beat. We don't need you to have a medical event too."

I suck in a breath, the dusty air tickling my nose before lodging in my chest, tightly coiled. Shallow.

"Accidents like this are part of the job." Colt is still caging me with his arm, though more loosely now. "Levi knows that. Shit like this happens sometimes."

I spin in his grip and meet his gaze, fire building behind my tongue. "You, of all people, don't get to tell me what Levi *knows*. He's aware of the risks of this work. But this 'shit happens' nonchalance you're pulling right now? Go to hell. Are *you* aware of how hard he's worked for this? What he's given up for this opportunity? The . . . the choices he's made to court *your* favor?"

"He's green, Ana. He's going to get knocked around, and of course he's trying to stay close to me. That's how this works. Smart man."

"They're putting him on a stretcher, Colt. He's seriously hurt. Have a little empathy." I place both palms on his chest and push. Hard. With a slight stumble, he steps back and releases me from his grip. His eyes search mine, perceiving me, and the intensity of it makes my stomach turn.

"Ah, I get it now." He smirks. "You and Levi—you care about him. I knew you weren't that good of an actress."

"What we are to each other is none of your fucking business."

"Noted." He holds his palms up in surrender. "But when you're ready, you can send your thank-you gift to my trailer for planting the story that launched this whole charade. I know my role here."

"Planting the story? Why the fuck would *you* start a rumor that you were cheating on your wife?"

"What did I have to lose? No one blames the men."

Everything clicks into place: He was willing to risk whatever he had left with Francesca. That's how badly he wanted me out. Blood flows hot to my extremities. "Colt—with all my heart—go to hell."

I turn and watch the medical team load Levi into the back of the ambulance. They're working quickly, and while it gives me peace knowing they're doing what they need to do for him, I'd feel much less frantic if this seemed like less of an emergency.

The back door of the rig closes. I watch a paramedic bring down the latch and bang on the window to signal they're ready to go. It's a muffled *thump* of a sound, like hitting a knee on a wooden table. Red and blue strobes whirl to life, and the set goes quiet when their sirens start to blare. The last thing I experience of Levi, in this moment, is the screeching of tires peeling away from me.

"Let's keep filming," Francesca shouts as the vehicle

turns onto the main road. The cast and crew, who had been milling around, eating snacks, rubbernecking—the way people do when an incident doesn't make their world stop turning—circle up around her. "I want to praise all of you for the quick work of getting out of the way so we could get Levi loaded up quickly. Medical says he's breathing on his own, and we'll update you as we know more."

That coiled, shallow breath begins to seep lower in my lungs. My shoulders fall an inch from where I've been holding them.

He's breathing.

That's good.

Right?

Except it doesn't feel good. It feels like I'm being electrocuted, with each *what if* a jolt of pain that singes the nerves beneath my skin, hot and sharp. What if he's paralyzed or has a brain injury? What if he can't work again? What if he stays unconscious?

*What if this is my fault?*

After ignoring him for days, I decided to talk to him before the scene. I was awkward and noncommittal about meeting for dinner. I distracted him when he needed to be locked in, and now he's paying the price. My throat tightens again.

Francesca's voice interrupts my thoughts. "Everybody, back to one. Colt and Ana, hair and makeup is waiting to touch you up. Thanks, all."

I get halfway to the makeup chair before I turn around.

It's a conscious decision to honor a gravitational pull in the opposite direction, away from the cameras.

"Actually, I'm out," I shout at the AD, at Colt, at my poor makeup artist who's confused as hell, and to Francesca standing farther back, analyzing angles for the shot. "I'm going to the hospital. I'd say I'm sorry, but truthfully? I'm not. You can plan on me arriving at call time tomorrow, ready and eager to continue filming. But today, I'm done."

I'm halfway to the street when I realize I'm still in full costume. Gauzy, scratchy muslin draped over my shoulders, dragging on the ground like a bridal train. At least I have shoes on.

A Hyundai pulls up, and I rip open the door and throw myself inside. "Hannah?"

"Close enough."

The Uber app shows twenty-one minutes from here to Vanderbilt University Medical Center—the adult emergency room, not the children's hospital from our event.

"Any chance you can speed?"

"Nah, can't do that. But I can let you choose the music?"

"Whatever you want. Just go, please."

It's a five-star ride: The driver doesn't say another word, and we make it to the hospital in twenty.

The fluorescent lights humming in Levi's room are as startling as the antiseptic smell. At triage, when I barged in and demanded to see him, they told me he'd just gone to imaging. They probably shouldn't have, but either the woman at the desk felt bad for me or someone pulled some strings because I was quickly shown to a room missing its hospital bed.

Now I'm sitting in a plastic chair that creaks every time I move and shivering against the air conditioning blowing from above. The rush to get here is gone, and with it, the channel for my nervous energy. It's easy to take fear and propel it into action. It's a lot harder to sit with it, in it, and wait. I tap my fingers on my thighs. I tap my shoes on the linoleum. I turn over in my head what I might say when he returns, and what he might look like.

What do you say to the person you thought you were falling in love with—and then broke up with—who then gets gravely injured?

And what if he's not conscious to hear it?

The scrape of the glass door sliding open has me on my feet instantly. Two nurses begin to back Levi's bed through the triage room door, and I realize he may not know I'm here. He may not *want* me here.

"Move!" a man in starched blue scrubs shouts, gruff and commanding, as I scramble out of the way.

"Is he going to be OK?" I beg.

The nurse looks me up and down. "Wife or sister?" My gaze is trained on Levi, who is concerningly still, save for the brief twitch of a grimace.

"Oh, um, I'm a friend. Girlfriend? A coworker."

"If you're not family, I can't provide updates. Who let you back here?"

"Please, I just need to know if he'll be OK. That's all." My eyes rake over Levi's face, cataloging the scratches, the bruise on his right cheek, the bump protruding over his eyebrow.

"Ana?" Levi's attempt at my name comes out on a groan. It's groggy, like he has a mouth full of marbles. "Ana?" This time, one eye lifts half-open. The stiff fear pulsing through my body starts to dissipate.

"That's me, I'm Ana." I look to the nurse. "See, he wants me here." I make pleading eyes at Levi, and he gives me the smallest, slowest head nod as they place the blood pressure cuff back on his arm.

The nurse looks me over again and shrugs. I grab the chair and drag it to the edge of his bed, taking a seat for whatever tests he has—we have—ahead.

I watch as Levi engages his abs to try to sit up. He woke up again after a round of X-rays, just before a neurological exam. When he did, he grabbed my hand, and I haven't let go since.

"Easy there, cowboy."

"You know, I think calling me cowboy is even worse

now that I've been thrown off a horse," he replies with a sharp intake of breath, the kind someone takes when something—everything—hurts. "Are you insulting my skills? Or is that *sarcasm*, and if so, where's my signature Ana Barlow eye roll?"

"Glad to see your personality is still intact, but please, tell me where the pain is so I can call the nurse."

"You should see the other guy." He adjusts his position in bed, and his face twists with a wince. "Speaking of, is Nesbitt OK? I hope I didn't bang him up in the fall."

"Levi, Nesbitt is twelve hundred pounds of pure muscle. He banged you up and trotted away like it was nothing."

"I'll heal just fine."

This man, bloodied and bruised, with dirt matted in his hair, is trying to convince me all of this is just another workday. He attempts to contort his mouth into a smile, or something approximating it, before pain pulls his lips back from his teeth.

I move my chair even closer and bring my hand to his hair, freeing a small twig from it. "Do you remember what you said to me, once?"

He shakes his head. "I've said a whole lot to you, sweetheart."

The endearment, and the feeling behind it, pinches at my heart. Needles at the part of me I've tried to seal shut.

"*Your reality isn't a burden.* That's what you said to me that night of the tornado warning when we were talking about my bruises. Your reality isn't a burden to me, Levi. I wouldn't be here if it was. It's OK if you're not OK."

"You came all the way here and stayed all afternoon just to tell me it's OK if I'm not OK?"

"No, I'm here because I needed to see you. I left set because we were supposed to talk, and I was supposed to apologize, and then you went and got yourself flung off a horse. Honestly, if you didn't want to hang out with me, you could have just said so." What was supposed to be a chuckle at the end of my sentence comes out choked.

His eyes meet mine, vulnerable. "Wait—they didn't wrap for the day? You left set in the middle of filming to be here? After I wasn't honest about Colt?"

"I left because I couldn't physically bear the thought of staying behind." I clear my throat and bring my hand back to his, sliding it gently under his palm to avoid the IV threaded into his skin. "I left because I think this . . . what we have, or had . . . is fixable. The idea that I might not have the chance to fix it, that something could happen to you before I got the opportunity—it wasn't something I could live with. So I'm here."

He nods before pushing his fingers through mine. "You can go back, if you want. Now that you see I'm going to live. We don't have to talk now if they're waiting for you to film."

I give him his eye roll. "What I realized on the way here is that I don't care. I don't care if the crew is mad at me, or if the tabloids print something about me 'storming off set.' And until now, that's been the only thing I've ever cared about—making sure I look a certain way and act a certain way so I can control perception. But as I was running to meet the Uber . . ."

"*You* took an *Uber*?" Levi is incredulous.

"Yes, Levi, I took a fucking Uber because I realized, for the first time in my life, I have something I care about more than controlling what people think of me. I also realized that while calling you selfish for keeping what Colt said to yourself, I was selfish for expecting you to share it. I . . . I don't want to be selfish with my heart anymore."

"Sweetheart, that's a lot for me to take in right after a concussion." He gives me a wink that makes me want to smother him, or at least press my body flush against his. Levi has always known how to diffuse my big feelings with well-placed levity, even during that very first date at the gym, like he somehow knew me before he *knew* me. What a gift it is to be known.

"Thank you for being here." His voice turns serious. "I . . . God, I was so glad to see you. I want to apologize too, and I want to do it right. Can we do that?"

"We don't have to do anything right now. I don't need anything from you other than the knowledge that you're OK."

"Promise not to fake date the backup they bring in to replace me?" Levi's hand grips mine tighter, and I laugh at the absurdity of how we got here and with hope for the promise of where we could go. The way he fights a chuckle and his chest stutters under the weight of his visible joy, even while in a hospital bed, has warmth flooding my veins and wrapping around my heart. I twist my pinky finger around his.

## NASHVILLE LIFESTYLE DAILY NEWSLETTER

### Not So Fake? Ana Barlow Abandons Filming for Injured Levi Stephens

By Camille Stockton

According to several sources who spoke on the condition of anonymity, it's crunch time for *Athena's War* as the cast and crew plan to wrap up filming next week.

So why, then, was lead actress Ana Barlow spotted fleeing the set in the middle of a workday, still dressed as Athena, as she climbed into a rideshare? While we haven't been able to confirm the nature of the incident, rumor has it that stuntman—and Barlow's alleged fake boyfriend—Levi Stephens was injured while filming a scene on horseback.

Perhaps their relationship isn't so fake.

# XXV

## LEVI

I knock on the large wooden door. It's still ninety degrees and an hour until sunset, and my sweat glands notice. Or maybe it's my nerves. I shake out my arms and roll my head to expel some of the pent-up energy pulsing through my body.

"Levi! What a surprise!" Emily opens the door and speaks in a voice that is obnoxiously, suspiciously loud. She winks as she ushers me inside, then whispers, "I wanted to make sure she heard me."

"I'm confident she did." I laugh. Somehow, all the trouble I've had from being in cahoots with Ana, and then I guess with Colt, didn't stop me from scheming with Emily to have Ana ready for *something* at 7 p.m., dressed in whatever, hungry enough but not hangry.

"Levi's here?" Ana turns the corner to the foyer and stops. My right hand comes up for a wave, and her face goes soft as she takes in my chinos and button-down shirt. It's the same outfit from that first day at her home in LA, though I'm not sure she remembers. The bouquet of hydrangeas is a new addition, as is the sling cradling my left arm to stabilize my broken collarbone.

"What are you . . . ? Wait, you look so handsome." She stutters her way through the compliment as I move closer to her.

"And you look beautiful." I gesture with the flowers and let my hand linger on her arm as she takes them from me.

"I'm wearing jeans and a crop top." She waves me off. "There's not somewhere we're supposed to be tonight for the film, is there?" Her voice rises in pitch. "Hey, Em! There's not—"

I interject before Emily can answer. "No, no. I'm hoping you'll go on a date with me."

"You're asking me on a date?"

"Yep. Edwin's waiting for us outside, and you know we can't disappoint him."

"Of course not. Um, let me change."

"Don't."

The corners of her mouth turn up. "Well, I'll throw on some lipstick or something. Just a second."

Emily appears from the pantry with a vase in hand. "All systems go," she whispers with a pat on my shoulder.

On a quaint street across from Belmont University, Athens Family Restaurant is flanked by an international market and Mexican cantina, both of which are bustling with college students. Edwin drops us off out front, and the feel of Ana's hand in mine as we approach the front door settles some of the nervous energy buzzing under my skin. When the host welcomes us inside, the atmosphere is sparse, with exposed brick and hardwood floors. Still cozy. And the place is empty, just as planned.

Ana tilts her head to survey the space, and her eyes land on the table in the corner with a white tablecloth. "Where is everyone?"

"For our first real date, I wanted it to be just you and me. We've had plenty of time in front of other people."

"So you rented out a restaurant?"

I feel myself blushing. "It's the spot I suggested we visit on the day of the accident. And also a spot I could afford with my first-big-role stuntman salary."

"This is . . ." Ana squeals and wraps both arms around my waist, squeezing tight. "Wait! Sorry!" She lets go and brings a hand to my sling. "Did I hurt you?"

I slide my good arm around her and drag her back to me, pulling her against my chest and hips. The contact makes me want more. "I'm perfectly fine, promise. You like it?"

"I love it."

"Then let me just grab this." I pull out a chair and gesture for her to sit. "No menus tonight. They're going to bring us a bit of everything."

"You planned all of this?"

"I've found myself with some unexpected free time now that I'm not filming."

"Just trying to fill it then."

I settle into my chair and prop my good elbow on the table. "No, just trying to find a way to show someone who showed up for me that I'm here for her too."

"Uh-huh." She reaches for her glass. "So it's a reciprocal gesture." She pokes her tongue into the side of her cheek to hide a smile that wants to peek through. It's a put-on coy act to make it seem like she doesn't know exactly what she's doing. She's challenging me; she wants me to say out loud that I want her. I'll play along.

"Nah, I'm done with favors. No more 'You scratch my back, and I'll scratch yours' for me. Too transactional, and frankly, too risky."

"Is that so?"

A waiter approaches with a platter in each hand, overflowing with gyros, souvlaki, spanakopita, falafel . . . also what looks like a bacon cheeseburger, but I'm not here to question the chef.

"You were saying?" Ana asks while unspooling her silverware and placing the blue-and-white napkin on her lap. Then, watching me struggle to navigate my cutlery with my one good hand, she reaches across the table to assist.

"What *was* I saying?" My foot finds hers and gives it a playful nudge. She nudges back to say, *I'm waiting.*

I press my palm against the starchy fabric on my thighs to dry the evidence of my nerves. "At the hospital, when you said, 'I don't want to be selfish with my heart anymore'? I haven't stopped thinking about that. Because I don't want to be selfish with my heart anymore, either. I want to be free with it, but to be honest, I'm scared."

Ana reaches for my hand and pushes her fingers through mine, her thumb tracing shapes on my skin. We're back to the day we met, when she saw my fear and coaxed me out of it with her assurance and her touch. She made me feel brave that day. She's making me feel brave now.

"You and me, we don't respond the same way when we're scared," I say.

She nods and holds my gaze.

"You claim your ground and build a wall around yourself, so no one can get in. I do the opposite—I run. I ran to LA so I wouldn't have to face my parents' disappointment, and then when everything blew up with Colt, I ran from you to avoid yours."

"Levi, I want you to know—" Ana starts, but I interrupt her.

"Please, let me say this. I spent years running. I convinced myself that leaving is kind, because people are better off without me making their lives complicated. But then you showed up at the hospital—and it was the first time anyone's come after me. I screwed up, and I disappointed you, and you showed up anyway. And that made me want to stop running."

"So you're letting me catch you?" She tiptoes her nails up my forearm. It tickles, like sparks dancing on my skin.

"I'm already caught. I've been caught, if I'm honest, since the day you decided I was going to be yours—fake or not."

"I do like to stake a claim, don't I?" A warm flush tints the skin of her cheeks, her chest.

"It's one of my favorite things about you. You know what you want, and you do what it takes to get it. You're like Athena that way."

She takes the napkin from her lap and swats me with it playfully. "Ah, yes, 'the maiden goddess,' able to live life according to her own desires, not bound by societal expectations. That sounds like me." She's being sarcastic, but it's the most accurate summation of Ana Barlow I've ever heard. "Levi, I've spent my entire life trying to be perceived as someone I'm not. Societal expectations are the framework I operate within. They're the road map for everything I do."

"I hear you, but I'm not sure that's true anymore. You might not see it, but I do. You're here in jeans. You walked off set last week. If the rumors are true, you gave Colt a piece of your mind, and I haven't seen you look around once to figure out if there's a camera near the restaurant. You are eating food that has *cheese* and spending time with me because you want to, not because someone expects you to or because it might benefit your image." I count off my points on my good hand until I run out of fingers. "And those walls you put up, the ones you use to keep you safe and keep people at a distance? You let me inside them."

She sniffles and blinks in response, trying to shut down the wetness that's gathering at her lashes, under her nose.

"Damn it, Levi." She brings the napkin to her face and dabs it below her eyes before fanning herself with it. "You could've just said you're sorry, and I would've been thrilled, you know."

"I am sorry for hurting you. I'm sorry for any tears that day, or after. I'm not sorry for these, though, because you deserve to hear how incredible you are, even if it makes you cry. I'm going to keep telling you too, so get used to it."

"What was it you said during our pizza-making date? 'Don't start something you can't finish?'" She taunts with misty eyes.

I lean forward, pulling her gaze. "Oh, we're starting *and* finishing. And I'm going to do it right. Since you asked last time, it's my turn tonight: Will you be my girlfriend?"

"Yes. But for real this time." Ana gives me a wet and shaky smile. I pull my chair to her side of the table and set my good arm around her, my palm finding her shoulder and my thumb brushing the spot I love behind her ear. She melts into me at the contact. "You know, the press is really going to have a field day with this development."

"You mean the public won't understand that our fake relationship to cover up unfounded infidelity rumors wasn't a ploy to get back at Colt for his scheme to fire you? And that somewhere along the line we developed real feelings for each other? Yeah, that's all . . . a lot."

"I don't care about them getting it right. Only making sure that *we* do."

"And what does 'getting it right' look like? I want to take notes."

She steadies herself with a lungful of air and pulls her bottom lip between her teeth, thinking. "I want us to be honest about what's going on in our lives. I want lazy mornings in bed and evenings making pizza when we're back in LA. I want us to push back when the other is being self-deprecating. I want us to prioritize each other, knowing we'll make mistakes, but also that we can fix them if we're willing to be vulnerable. And I want us to fight for each other, not put up walls or run away when things get hard."

"I'm in." I bring my lips to Ana's hair and press a kiss to the top of her head. "You know, this reminds me of the list you rattled off the first day we met, with the rules for the arrangement. We broke one."

"The nothing-more-than-kissing one?" She tilts her head up to meet my gaze, a mischievous smile curling her lips. Below the table she puts her hand on my thigh.

"Hmm, yeah, OK. Two. The kissing one, and also your last one."

"And what was that?"

"About me not falling in love with you."

Her grin is coy. "I seem to remember you saying it wouldn't be a problem. You were *very* sure of that." She drums her fingertips on my leg, a reassurance tapped in code.

"I didn't stand a chance."

The action continues: For the exclusive on Ana and Levi's future together, read the epilogue and dive into the world of *Athena's War*. Just scan below or visit 831stories.com/doublestandard.

# ACKNOWLEDGMENTS

One of the sweetest pictures of my grandparents shows them in black and white, sitting on the steps of Nashville's Parthenon in 1952. They were just married and new to town, courtesy of the US Air Force. "Bud and his favorite girl" is written on the back of the photo. They lived a few blocks from the Parthenon for just two months before Bud deployed and Mary Ann moved back to Ohio—closer to her family in St. Sebastian, the same tiny hometown I gave Levi Stephens.

My first thanks belongs to my Grandpa Bud, who at ninety-seven years old gave me the full history of how their story compares to Ana and Levi's: young love, a brief stint in town for work, with family left behind in a small farming community. I hadn't considered any of this when I started writing *Double Standard* (it was originally set in LA!), but perhaps it's kismet, because my ability to craft romance exists in part from their modeling—sixty years of happy marriage. My grandma would be tickled by all of this. I have to believe she is thrilled from where she sits on the other side.

Next, thank you to Erica Cerulo and Claire Mazur for recognizing the promise in this idea when it was only two chapters and a *very* rough outline. Your support and encouragement were life-giving throughout this process, and I couldn't be more proud to be part of the 831 Stories family!

To Callie Deitrick and Wendy Sherman, the best agents in the biz—thank you for shepherding me through this process, for answering my anxious emails, and for handling my occasional breakdowns and indecision with such patience and grace. I wouldn't want anyone else on my team.

To Georgia Clark, Madison Feller, and Sanjana Basker, who helped shape the story with their thoughtful edits and constructive suggestions. The book is so much better as a result of your feedback!

To Catherine Krenzer for being an ardent supporter of my work, both for 831 Stories and personally. You're a gem, and I'm so glad for the chance to work together.

To my best friend, Sara, who read my second draft and assured me it wasn't awful when I was very sure it was.

I say it in every acknowledgments list, and I will continue to until the end of time: Thank you to my husband, Tyler, who has never once treated my wild and impulsive ideas as silly. Thank you for taking the kids so I can write and edit and market and just generally have too much stuff on my plate. Thank you for believing that it's important for the kids to see me dreaming big and achieving those dreams. Thank you for speaking my name with pride and awe in every room you enter. I love you. I got the best one.

To T. and M., I love that you love that your mom is an author. Your encouragement means everything. Thank you for sharing me with my stories. May you also go after whatever wild and impulsive thing your heart leads you toward. I love you.

To the rest of my family, who have to answer questions about their loved one taking a hard pivot to become a smutty romance author but who do it joyfully anyway—thank you for buying my books, recommending my books, reviewing my books, coming to my events, and never discussing the spicy parts with me. You make it so easy to love and be loved. I'm the luckiest.

Thank you, readers and reviewers, Bookstagrammers and BookTokers, Thriends and author colleagues for making this work worth it. It's a tough industry, and connecting with y'all is one of the very best parts.

And to you, specifically, who's still reading this—thank you for picking up *Double Standard* and spending your precious time with it. I hope you had a fun and joyful few hours in Levi and Ana's world! If you loved it, please rate and review it on Goodreads and Amazon. This is the best gift you can give any author, as it helps the algorithm recommend the book to others who might enjoy it.

Thank you, thank you. I couldn't be more grateful.

# ABOUT THE AUTHOR

Mallory Thomas is a writer and reader of soft love stories that make you swoon, squeal, and blush. *Double Standard* is her third rom-com, joining *Somewhere Along the Line* and *Untangled* (which you should definitely read). When she's not writing, she can be found picking up after her two kids, joking with her handsome husband, and planning trips to the beach. She's also a baby formula expert and content creator.

# ALSO FROM 831 STORIES

### *Big Fan* by Alexandra Romanoff

A high-profile scandal derailed Maya's DC career, and she's eager to fly under the radar—that is, until her former boy-band crush reaches out with a job offer.

### *Hardly Strangers* by A.C. Robinson

One night with a rock star could upend Shera's best-laid plans, revealing how a chance encounter can rewrite a story—and change everything.

### *Comedic Timing* by Upasna Barath

Naina is seeking a fresh start in NYC after breaking up with her girlfriend, but when she meets someone at a party, he's so offtype that her attraction to him fuels an identity crisis.

### *Set Piece* by Lana Schwartz

When a breakout BBC star gets swarmed by fans during a night out, it's a no-nonsense bartender, CJ, who rescues him—and warms them both up for an after-hours hookup.

### *Square Waves* by Alexandra Romanoff

The first spin-off in the *Big Fan* series, an enemies-to-lovers romance in which tabloid fodder mixes with a long-brewing rivalry as Cassidy contends with her high-school nemesis.

### *Exit Lane* by Erika Veurink

A postcollege cross-country road trip sparks *something* between Marin and Teddy—though it's not quite clear what. Over the next eight years, they have fated encounters on multiple continents.

### *Grape Juice* by Eliza Dumais

When Alice lands in France for a wine harvest, she's disenchanted with her life. But she soon finds something she's missing in the vineyard owner's nephew Henri, who's just as lost as she is.

### *Rooting Interest* by Cat Disabato

When Felix gets pulled off her NFL beat to cover the WNBA, she doesn't expect to find herself so taken with the sport—or with one of its biggest stars, Natalie Czapski.

### *Found Time* by Caroline Goldstein

Lili and Reid lock eyes after a 1993 Jeff Buckley show. Thirty years and a whole lifetime later, they cross paths once more. Can they finally make their way back to each other?

### *Major Gift* by Tiffany Ezuma

Ndidi, the widow of a billionaire tech mogul, is determined to give her wealth away—and keep one secret from Geoffrey, the perceptive journalist tasked with telling her story.

### *Down to Earth* by Julia Turshen

Vegetable farmer Frankie doesn't know what to make of Paige, the Brooklyn mom who's moved to her quiet upstate town. But could the attraction she's feeling grow into something more?

# 831 STORIES BOOK CREDITS

So many people were involved in bringing this book to life. Many of their names are included here, but there would be no HEA without the passionate work of booksellers and librarians and the enthusiasm of readers. And as we all know, romance readers are the best readers.

### 831 Stories

Erica Cerulo, Madison Feller, Marie Joh, Catherine Krenzer, Claire Mazur, Elaine Orihuela, Angela Vang

### Authors Equity

Andrea Bachofen, Rose Edwards, Carly Gorga, Sarah Christensen Fu, Becca Kadison, Deb Lewis, Madeline McIntosh, Nina von Moltke, Diana Simmons, Erin Vandeveer, Don Weisberg, Craig Young

## C47 Design

Phil Chang, Haneu Kang, Jamin Lee, Naomi Otsu, Sunny Park

## Editing

Sanjana Basker, Georgia Clark, Meaghan O'Connell

## Marketing, Events, and Publicity

Emma Benshoff, Zoë Gillespie, Tara Larsen, Ashleigh Magee, Kaitlin Phillips, Riley Vaske, Kristin White

## Production

Sam Martin, Scribe Inc.

Keep reading for a taste of

*Rooting Interest*

by Cat Disabato

from 831 Stories

# 1

Stepping into the arena, I feel a familiar crackle. The air sizzles like it's charged with electricity, like in the moments before a thunderstorm breaks.

The final few minutes before a game begins is my favorite thing about sports. It doesn't matter if the setting is a barely groomed field in a hidden corner of a suburb or a brand-new, state-of-the-art, $200 million facility in a major city. The feeling is always the same: anticipation, suspense, but most of all, possibility. Any team could come out on top. Any player could have the night of their life. The goals are specific and simple: play well; win. Off the field it isn't so simple, but that hardly matters here. Nothing gets me down in these moments. No matter how far I've drifted off course.

I'm supposed to be on the familiar sidelines of an NFL practice field, developing a rapport with Los Angeles Cougars rookies and coaxing quotes out of the coaching staff. While the guys ready their bodies and their plays during training camp, I am supposed to be filing stories about the new football season for the *LA Chronicle*. Instead, that beat—*my* beat, the one I fought for through innumerable late nights and with ruthless competence—has been plucked out of my grasp, as if it'd never really been mine at all.

For reasons too painful to consider closely—namely, that I am the sports section's only queer female staff writer—my editor reassigned me to cover WNBA All-Star weekend in Phoenix. I'm here because of my repeated requests to write more features, my editor, David, insisted, but the features I'd been pitching him were about football. Imagine my surprise when the response to my pitch about the Cougars' offensive weaknesses was an assignment to cover Natalie Czapski, the star player for the Hollywood Lights, and her comeback after an ACL injury.

I've never written about basketball. I've hardly ever watched it. But now, a scant few hours after booking my travel and scrambling to make my flight, I am going to have to figure it out. Even if the ground beneath my feet feels no more solid than sand.

At least the energy in the PHX Arena is familiar, the excitement sparking the air, boosting my mood and calming my anxiety as I wind my way through the crowd. Fans who look like they've been following their team for decades mix with overstimulated kids, couples holding hands, and chattering groups of friends. All-Star weekend means people are decked out like the color spectrum: red for the Las Vegas Aces, seafoam for New York Liberty, and burgundy for the Lights. In my usual work outfit of a black button-down and black pants, I fade into the background, just as intended.

I try hard not to come off as anyone or anything in particular when I'm on the job. To ticket holders, the press badge around my neck means I'm someone official, and to players, I'm nothing outside of my game knowledge and the questions I ask them—more of a conduit than a person. It's something I learned from David, who was David Greenebaum, sportswriting legend, before he was my mentor and my first-name-basis boss. Now that I am unexpectedly in a position of having to win back a job that I thought was mine, following David's lead—playing by his rules—is more crucial than ever.

When I make my way to press row, I'm mildly surprised to discover that it's right behind the announcers' table, close enough that I'll probably hear their commentary. I find my assigned seat between a young Black guy, who gives me a tight smile with "no new friends" energy, and a white person with a dyed-pink mohawk and, helpfully, a "they/them" pronouns pin.

They look at my badge, then my face, then my badge again. "Wow, is the *LA Chronicle* finally covering the WNBA? Or is this just for Nat's comeback?"

The small placard in front of them identifies them as a freelancer, someone used to being batted around by whatever publication decides to say yes to a pitch. And they clearly know that covering women's sports is still seen as optional at most big outlets.

I know how to play this. I shrug and say, "I go wherever they tell me to go."

They stick out their hand. "Danny."

"Jennifer Felix," I say, shaking it. "But everybody calls me Felix."

As I busy myself plugging my computer into the power strip taped to the table, Danny makes conversation. "It'll be good to have CZ back in the four spot."

It's like they're speaking in a foreign language that I studied in high school, some vocabulary familiar but the full extent of the meaning lost on me.

"Totally," I say.

"Or do you think she'd do better in the five?" Danny asks mildly.

"She's, um, I think she's got something to prove so she'll step up in any role." It's not like I've said anything wrong. The problem is, I haven't said anything at all. When sportswriters talk, we argue about minutiae and one-up each other with niche facts and hot takes. I can tell from Danny's raised eyebrow that they can see right through me, see how little I know.

"Oh, honey," Danny says, almost sympathetically, but with a vicious little edge. I wonder suddenly if they'd pitched a WNBA story to the *Chronicle*, gotten the feedback that there wasn't an audience, only now to see someone totally ignorant of the game plopped down next to them to cover it. "You're really fucked, aren't you." Not a question.

"I'm a fast learner," I say.

"You better be," they say, and pointedly turn back to their computer. Conversation over.

I'm rattled, and I know it shows. Determined to shake it off, I return to my setup, straighten my laptop, and shut down any application I don't need. Sports is a world full of rituals (or superstitions, to the nonbelievers); players have their lucky socks or listen to the same song before every tip-off. And I have mine. I close my eyes. I take deep breaths through my nose. I listen to the sounds of the crowd, note the scents in the arena. The voices aren't just energized; they're giddy, and much more high-pitched and femme than what I'm used to from NFL fans. I hear the squeak of rubber soles on the arena floor and heels on the stairs. I smell popcorn, ketchup, and Dove deodorant.

This cataloging is a practice I copied from David. He wrote a book called, simply, *Writing the Game*, which my father gave me for my sixteenth birthday. My copy is so dog-eared, underlined, and just generally run-through that it's falling apart at the binding. One of the lines I've committed to memory: "Attending a sports game as a fan is a five-pronged sensory experience, so writing about sports should be the same." One twisted bra strap digging into the skin of my shoulder is the last sensation I identify before opening my eyes. I slip my hand under my shirt and untwist it, making sure everything is in its right place. I'm as ready as I can be.

The announcer's voice booms, *"Welcome to All-Star weekend!"*

The screams of the crowd swell to a new crescendo as the announcer starts calling out the first few players, none of whose names I recognize. Cameras flash as the announcer rumbles, *"Back from a season-ending injury to show us what a Big can do in this competition, and representing the Hollywood Lights, it's CZ, Natalie Czapski!"*

In my rush to research three decades of WNBA history, I'd reduced Natalie to her component parts: her wingspan, her layup, the design of her Nike sneakers, the muscle she'd put on after her rookie year and the speed it gives her. In doing so, I somehow failed to understand what Natalie looked like as a whole. She glides onto the court, all long-limbed grace. Her blonde hair is pulled into tight French braids. On the Jumbotron, I can see how the turquoise blue accents on the Lights' uniform bring out the richness in her pale eyes. And how her big, crooked smile, which stretches across her whole face, makes her seem a little cocky—but also kinetic enough to power the sun. The way the tip of her tongue pokes out slyly between her teeth makes something hum in my rib cage.

She flexes her right bicep and laughs when the crowd goes even wilder. There's no way for me to hear her, but I can read her lips as she screams at them—at us: "LET'S FUCKING GO." My stomach and chest pulse with little bursts of want. Fuck. In my rush to get ready for this new assignment, I'd somehow forgotten that the WNBA is filled with my exact type: pretty tomboys with bravado. I'm pummeled by the unprofessional thought *Natalie Czapski is hot!!* I *never* had this problem in the NFL.

I can't afford distractions right now, so I turn my attention back to my notes. Tonight's the skills competition, followed by the three-point shooting contest, and I watch the first three players blaze through the stations, writing down their times for their exercises (39.2 seconds, 45.1 seconds, and an unfortunate 55.6 seconds).

I log any game vernacular that isn't immediately familiar to me in a section of my doc called "Terms and Lingo." For the Cougars, I have meticulously organized research and notes and quotes, everything at my fingertips and ready for me to draw on in an instant when inspiration either strikes or lacks so much that I need to rely on previously accumulated information. My new file has a "Questions" section that is twice as long as the rest of the document, filled with inquiries that I'm sure are mind-numbingly basic to even casual fans. Things like "What does it mean to 'space the floor'?" and "Where did Natalie Czapski go to high school?"

As I type, fast without looking at the screen, I watch Natalie in her seat, her infectious smile only disappearing when her jaw drops in awe as a contestant lands a neat three-pointer. Scanning the crowd, I see I'm in good company: Natalie's getting attention from all over the arena, everyone from former teammates who playfully squeeze her shoulder as they pass to a brunette sitting courtside in a handmade "CZ DOES IT" T-shirt. She is a magnet, drawing in focus and metabolizing it into charm.

When it's her turn, she strips off her warm-up jacket, springs on the balls of her feet, and shakes out her elegantly muscular arms. At the whistle, she's off like a rocket. This is when my years of sportswriting—even about an entirely different game—pay off. Some highly trained sliver of my brain automatically translates what she's doing on the court into dynamic language. She bounces passes into a row of progressively smaller nets, hitting her mark on the first try for each. She races toward the basket, sets up at the initial shoot zone, and drops her ball cleanly through the net. As she sinks the next, I note the way her fingertips graze the ball and the flex of her calves as she jumps with her shot. She's stunning to watch.

Natalie finishes her run with an easy layup and plants her hands on her thighs, her chest heaving with deep breaths as the announcer's voice booms out her impressive time: *28.2 seconds*. From the vibe of the arena, I can tell that no matter how the rest of the night goes for Natalie Czapski, she's shown everyone that she is *so* back.

She wins the skills competition—it isn't even close—and I take note of reporters buzzing around me. "That footwork—never would have known anything had ever been wrong with her knee," a guy with a buzz cut says. She could've stopped there and relaxed into the loose, playful atmosphere of All-Star weekend, but instead she goes into the three-point contest radiating the determination of someone with something to prove.

A player named Ruthie Jones makes enough three-point shots that it feels like no one can beat her, so when Natalie starts shooting, the crowd is loud and yammering, not paying much attention. But Natalie is doing even better than Ruthie, making more baskets than she's missing. The whole mass of us goes holding-our-breath quiet, falling into that calm that swoops in during a big play when it feels like an errant shout could disrupt the equilibrium and throw a player off.

"No," someone behind me whispers in awe. "She literally can't do it."

I glance back at the fan, two rows above and wearing a Czapski jersey; the Lights' logo, a playful riff on the Hollywood Walk of Fame stars, is nearly glowing on her shirt. The fan is squeezing her friend's hand, eyes locked to the court and sparkling. "She can't, she can't, she can't," the woman chants, but she's breathless in anticipation, using the negative to invoke the opposite: *She can, she can, she can.*

Next to me, Danny murmurs their own writing out loud, a copyediting trick to catch errors. "No player has ever won both the skills competition and three-point contest in the same WNBA All-Star weekend."

Natalie isn't just doing well; she might be setting a record. My own fingers fly over the keyboard as my eyes stay glued on her. She grabs her last ball, bends her knees, and shoots. It arcs balletically and slips cleanly through the basket. Even I know enough about this sport to think the word *swish*. The reverent hush gives way to explosive cheers. Natalie Czapski has made history.

I feel a flutter in my chest, the way I do when an article goes viral, like maybe this is less of a demotion than I thought. I could write a great piece here, especially if I trust that my storytelling skills are just as valuable as being a ball-knower. My uncertainty gives way to a more familiar feeling: determination. There is a good story to tell about Natalie, and I'm going to figure out how to tell it.

As I flash my badge to the security guy at the door of the media room, I hope I'm radiating "Can you believe this night?" buzz and not anxious "I'm new here" energy, but the feelings are a little muddled.

Basketball might be uncharted for me, but the organized chaos of this presser—press conference—is not. I'm intimately acquainted with the symphony of scuttling PR women backed by the frenetic clack of fingers on keyboards, the chaotic disarray of tangled laptop chargers and extension cords, broadcast camera people setting up their gear elbow to elbow. My eyes bounce off the smattering of old white dudes—they are everywhere in sports media, as pervasive as crabgrass—and slow to scan the faces that make me feel an unexpected sense of belonging. Even though I don't recognize anyone in the room, there is a surprising sense of the familiar in the people around me: a woman with a taper fade haircut, someone holding a laptop with "Protect trans kids" stickers, and a guy in the corner with a fully beat face. I can picture these people out at the dyke nights I go to in LA—just not at my sports bars. But here they are, with barely suppressed excitement to cover what turned out to be a momentous athletic event.

I find my seat in the second row. I start my voice recording and hope it doesn't catch my audible intake of breath when Natalie is ushered into the room. She was alluring from across the court. From less than six feet away, she's spellbinding.

I pull up the gamer on my laptop screen, the recap article that I need to publish as soon as possible, and while I review my stats and check the spelling of players' names, the reporters around me start asking questions.

"Natalie, congratulations. How does it feel to make history tonight?"

Like most professional athletes, she's been media trained into oblivion, giving the kind of basic, boring responses that allow beat writers to file their pieces and her to avoid controversy. It's standard stuff, nothing really inspiring. Tracking the patterns in the questions themselves is more interesting. We are supposed to be celebrating, but after that first question, everyone seems to have already moved past the significance of the moment on to the future of her game, asking about the pressure she faces, soliciting comments on how much is riding on her. I imagine my fellow reporters typing phrases like "crushing weight," "grim intensity," "tall hill to climb." I've made it as far as I have in my career by pushing into a story as far as it will give, and I sense there's something else we aren't getting here, something to be gleaned from that ever-present smile.

Natalie's night wasn't about proving something in the wake of her injury, I'm realizing as I take her in. It was about the joy of playing the game. This is a narrative I can weave without knowing all that much about basketball; I just need a good quote from her to make the piece work.

"We have time for one more," the team publicist says, and my hand shoots in the air faster than anyone else's.

"There, on the left."

"Hi, Jennifer Felix, *LA Chronicle*," I respond, pushing aside the flicker of warmth pooling in my stomach when Natalie turns her attention to me. "You looked like you were having a lot of fun out there. Were you having fun?"

"Yeah, I was having a great time out there. Anytime I get to be on a basketball court and playing, I'm happy."

*Anytime I get to be on a basketball court and playing, I'm happy.* It's a good kicker. I nod. "Thank you!" I respond.

Natalie's smile drops, and with a jolt I realize she doesn't see what I'm after. And that the version of her that radiates brightness has a darker flip side, a stone wall that blocks out the light.

"That's it?" Her voice is teasing, but not breezy. There

is a real bite in her tone. "That's your question? Did you really just ask me if I *enjoy* playing basketball?"

"I wanted to hear about how you felt on the court tonight," I answer uneasily, the warmth in my core replaced by a sinking feeling.

"Do you have a basketball question? Because I have some basketball things to talk about." She rests her elbows on the table and leans forward, homing in on me.

Watching this on playback, a casual observer probably wouldn't read anything into our exchange because of Natalie's careful tone. They wouldn't be able to see the way Natalie's eyes lock on mine and the fact that there's no give in them, no humor at all. Her stare is a razor-edged challenge, a test I know I'm going to fail. I can't ask a basketball question because it will reveal that I don't know what I'm talking about, but if I don't ask a basketball question . . . it will also reveal that I don't know what I'm talking about.

"That's it from me," I say, hoping she'll let it die.

She doesn't.

She leans back in her chair, folds her arms across her chest. "I haven't seen you before. Do you know the league?"

I want to tell her that watching her play made me more emotional—felt more visceral—than a sporting event has in years. But that's not something a journalist can say, so instead I give her four words that couldn't be more passionless: "I'm working on it."

Her eyes narrow. “Working on it,” she parrots, pushing back her chair. “Well, thanks for trying, I guess. Goodnight, everybody.” Then she walks out of the room, never looking back. I watch her go, shock giving way to anxiety and then painful, red-hot embarrassment.